Lassie

TREASURE HUNTER

Lassie—originated by MGM
Authorized edition featuring characters from
the Lassie television program

By

CHARLES S. STRONG

Illustrated by

HARRY L. TIMMINS

WHITMAN PUBLISHING COMPANY
RACINE, WISCONSIN

PRINTED IN U.S.A.

Treasure! It was a magic word that sounded the beginning of high adventure for Lassie and her young master, Timmy. With their pal, Boomer, they were to discover that treasure-hunting could be the most exciting and the most dangerous pastime in the whole world.

And as if Indian treasure were not enough, there was the bank robbery in Capitol City to think about too! Lassie had helped to capture one of the bandits, and it soon became evident that the hunt for ancient treasure might lead to the criminals and modern treasure as well. There was clearly a mysterious connection between the happenings on Lookout Mountain and the eighty-thousand-dollar robbery.

Timmy and Boomer found the answers the hard way. Trapped in a cave, with only a skeleton for company, they might never have lived to tell their story if it hadn't been for Lassie. Once again the great dog proved her intelligence, loyalty, and marvelous courage—and proved herself the finest treasure hunter of all.

Contents

1 SUMMER PLANS

Lassie was resting in the shade of the summerhouse where the green grapes hung heavily on the vines. It was a warm afternoon in June. The big collie was half asleep, but she sensed everything going on about the Martin farm.

Through the open window she could hear Ruth Martin singing a pleasant tune as she put pies into the oven. Several pies were on the window sill cooling. The warm tang of the apples came to Lassie, and her mouth watered.

The piglets in the sty grunted as they played near the sow, splashed in the mud, or slipped and slid in the feed trough. Chickens, pecking in the hard ground of the barnyard, looked at the resting collie now and then.

Down at the barn, Uncle Petrie was busy. A loud *clang-g-g* came to Lassie as the old man beat on an iron wagon wheel rim with a blacksmith's hammer.

Now and then Lassie lifted her head from her forepaws and looked across a field toward where the Martin cows were grazing. Some of them were milk cows, and their calves ran with them. Others were beef cattle which Uncle Petrie and Paul Martin were fattening for meat. Lassie spent part of her time herding the cattle, and she felt they were her cows.

All of these things were important to Lassie, but the sounds she most wanted to hear were those telling of the return of Timmy from school in town. The welcome cries were not long in coming. While Timmy was still a quarter of a mile away from the farmyard, coming up the dirt road on his bicycle, he began to call, "Lassie! Lassie!"

The big collie jumped up, shot out of the summerhouse like a shell from a cannon. She landed running on the dirt path and was down the road like a flash. As she raced along she barked happily, and no one could doubt that she was glad to see Timmy.

Timmy was used to this excited reception, but he always found it hard not to run down Lassie with his bicycle.

He stopped as the dog came dashing up and petted her happily. Then Lassie took her place beside the bicycle, and Timmy rolled along toward the house.

At the sounds of Lassie's barking, Ruth Martin came to the kitchen door and smiled at the boy and the dog. Timmy was laughing and talking, and Lassie nodded as though she understood every word.

"School is over for the summer, Lassie! Now I won't have to leave you alone every day. We can go fishing and hiking with Uncle Petrie and Boomer. We'll have a lot of fun!"

Lassie barked her agreement.

Ruth turned back indoors and Lassie and Timmy went on to the barn. Uncle Petrie came to meet them as Timmy put away his bicycle.

"What's all the excitement?" the old man asked.

"No more school!"

"They're the best days of your life, lad," Uncle Petrie said. "But you don't find it out until it's too late."

Timmy merely smiled. "See you later, Uncle Petrie," he cried. Then he called to Lassie and they both ran toward the house. The eager youngster was sniffing the smells that came from the kitchen. As he grabbed for the handle of the screen door, he shouted, "Pies! Apple pies and blueberry pies! *Ummm-yummm!*"

Lassie barked and sniffed. Ruth smiled pleasantly. Her face was bright with perspiration, several strands of her hair were on her forehead, but her eyes were filled with pride as she looked at her adopted son. Timmy filled a big spot in Ruth's life.

"Did you get promoted, son?" she asked, putting an arm around his shoulders.

"Sure thing," Timmy said briskly. "I'm going into the third grade."

"Good for you, Timmy." His mother hugged him, and Lassie brushed against her apron, looking up into her smiling eyes as if she did not like being ignored.

Mrs. Martin included Lassie in her embrace. Then she asked Timmy, "What are you fellows—er, *folks*—going to do now?"

Timmy chuckled. "It's hard to remember that Lassie is a lady, isn't it? She must be a tomboy, don't you think,

Mom? She acts like one."

"I guess she is," Ruth agreed. "But where are you going this afternoon?"

Timmy's eyes were glowing. "I'm changing into my old clothes, then Boomer is coming over with Mike. We're all going to dig for grubs at the edge of the pond. Tomorrow morning we're going down to the river and fish."

"Grubs?" Ruth repeated. "Well, don't get too dirty while you're doing it."

Timmy looked at his mother as though she just didn't understand boys. "Like Uncle Petrie says, if I get dirty, there's always plenty of washing water." He rushed off to his room with Lassie trotting along behind him.

Timmy's school clothes went flying in every direction, and he hurried into his work shirt and denim overalls. Lassie watched him for some moments, then began picking up the things from the floor and putting them on the bed.

Timmy grinned. "I guess you're right, Lassie," he said. "I'd better hang them up, or Mom won't like it."

The boy and the dog headed back through the kitchen. Timmy said good-by to his mother; then he and Lassie banged open the screen door and were on their way across the farmyard.

Boomer Bates was already on his way down the road on his bicycle as Timmy and Lassie came to the gate in the barnyard fence. Lassie greeted the neighbor boy with a loud bark, before turning her attention to Mike who was trotting along behind the bicycle. The Bates pet was a mixed-breed hunting dog. Boomer found him the most wonderful dog in the world in spite of Mike's unhappy look.

"Hi, Boomer!" Timmy greeted his pal. "Take the bike to the barn, then we'll all head for the pond."

While Boomer was putting away his bicycle, Timmy found a large bucket and two small shovels. Uncle Petrie greeted Boomer as he came into the barn, then stepped outside.

"You must be planning on a heap of grubs, from the size of that pail, son."

Timmy looked at the bucket. "We're figuring on a heap of fishing."

Boomer came hurrying back and Timmy handed him

one of the shovels. They waved to Uncle Petrie; then, with Lassie and Mike trotting along between them, they headed toward the tall trees beyond the Martin wood lot. On the far side there was a large pond.

The Martin pond added a lot to the life on the farm. Timmy had always liked it. As they came up, ducks were swimming along on its surface. Song birds were diving and flying from the trees overhead. Ruth had once told Timmy that the water made Nature's music when it was flowing through the gate at the dam to water the garden patch.

Uncle Petrie had opened the gate just before noon and would be coming to close it before supper. In between, the muddy edge of the pond would be a good spot to find hellgrammites, grubs, night crawlers, and other good fish bait.

Timmy and Boomer kicked off their shoes and were soon splashing barefooted in the water which was only about two feet deep at the rim of the pool. It would be easier for them to work from the water side than on the slippery mud. Lassie played in the water for a while, sending the ducks swimming to the other end of the pond. Mike had no intention of going for a swim. He hurried off into the woods, chasing rabbits.

When Lassie finished her first swim, she came up beside the boys and shook water all over them.

"Lassie! Lassie!" they shouted, as though they were really angry. They splashed water back on the dog with their hands and shovels. Lassie didn't like this game at all. There were large clots of mud on the shovels and they surprised the collie as they struck her. Timmy and Boomer turned back to their digging, picking the grubs out of the wet dirt on the spades and putting them into the bucket.

The dog watched the digging for a while. Then she stuck her nose into the bucket, sniffed loudly, and turned away.

"You can't eat them, Lassie," Timmy said and Boomer laughed. Lassie shook her head sharply, then barked agreement. She turned back into the water. Since Timmy and Boomer did not want to play with her, she would find something to do herself.

During the winter and spring months, while the pond

was frozen over, Lassie and Timmy had come down here with Uncle Petrie and Paul to break through the ice to get water to supply the stock. At the western end of the pond, near the dam gate, there had been a large muskrat village. During the cold months, when their fur was long and valuable, Uncle Petrie had showed Timmy how to set small traps for the muskrats. When they caught the muskrats and skinned them, Timmy kept a part of the money they brought for spending, but most of it went into the bank to send him to college.

Lassie had always liked to chase the little animals across the snow and ice. Now she headed down to look at the muskrat homes. Her sense of smell had told her long ago that the muskrats were gone for the summer. The straw, mud, and stick houses of the animals were now above water, because the dam gate had been opened to water the garden. Lassie walked around on top of the straw piles, then found one of the doorways and began to tear it apart with her strong forefeet.

The roof of the house was dry and stiff. The sticks broke in half as Lassie worked. A few of them flew through the air and splashed into the water. Some field mice had been living in the muskrat burrows, and they came running out to see who was wrecking their homes. Lassie did not bother them but went on digging.

Finally she was down to the bare ground. The soft dirt was easy to dig in, and she was enjoying her exercise. Suddenly her claws struck stones. She looked down at them and barked as though she did not like to be stopped. She dug some more, then rested, running her forepaws through the soft dirt before her. She barked again.

Timmy and Boomer looked up at the second bark. Timmy dropped a spadeful of mud into the grub bucket and called, "What is it, Lassie? What have you found?"

Lassie's answer was more barking. Timmy and Boomer knew that the muskrats were gone. Even if any of them were still in the straw village they would not be worth anything. Fur-bearing animals do not have good skins in the warm summer months. Uncle Petrie had explained that to them last spring.

"Let's go see," Boomer said.

At the approach of the boys, the collie ran along the

shore of the pond to meet them. Timmy dropped an arm around her neck, and they all went back to the village together. Even Mike followed, attracted by Lassie's barking. As they came toward the hole she had been digging, Lassie broke away from Timmy and jumped over the loose dirt. She spread her forelegs at the rim of the hole as if to protect what it held.

Timmy looked down at the spot where Lassie had been digging. It was about three feet square. "Look at this, Boomer!" he cried. "Come here, will you?"

Boomer and Mike hurried up and looked down into the hole.

"What is it, Timmy? I don't see anything but a lot of dirty old stones."

Timmy knelt in the soft dirt and reached down to the bottom of the hole. He brought up several of the stones. He carried them to the edge of the pond and splashed them in the water. When the dirt was washed off, he held them up. "They're Indian arrowheads. Uncle Petrie has some just like these in his old trunk. Maybe they had a big Indian battle around here. Boy, this is a real mystery!"

Boomer did not share the excitement of Timmy and Lassie. He sat down beside the hole while the boy and his dog ran back to the grub bucket for the shovels. Mike rested his muzzle on Boomer's lap and was content.

For the next ten or fifteen minutes, Timmy dug furiously in the hole which Lassie had begun. He found about twenty-five arrowheads, half a dozen spearheads, and a broken pottery dish.

"Boy," he cried, "wait until Uncle Petrie sees this! I'll bet he didn't know anything about it. Maybe we'll find out how they got here. Do you think it *was* an Indian battle, Boomer?"

Lassie knew she had brought real pleasure to Timmy, her beloved master, so she raced around happily. But Boomer wasn't so sure there was reason to get excited.

"It couldn't have been a very big battle with only twenty-five arrowheads," he said, looking over the collection.

Timmy pouted. "Well, I think it's the beginning of a big mystery. But we'll see what Uncle Petrie says."

Timmy decided that they had done enough digging for

the afternoon. He put some clean straw on top of the grubs in the pail and laid the Indian relics on the straw. He covered the muskrat village carefully, then hammered a stick into the ground with his shovel, so he could find the spot again if the pond water rose and flooded the village.

The boys climbed up to the level ground beside the pond and started for home. Boomer took one end of the bucket handle to show he felt this might really turn into a good thing and he wanted a share of it. Lassie jumped around the boys and Mike followed along more quietly.

"Don't tell anybody but our folks about what we found," Timmy said seriously. "I bet these things could make us famous. Besides we don't want people running all over Dad's farm and digging up the whole place."

"I can keep a secret," Boomer assured Timmy. "I won't tell anyone."

Lassie barked loudly to show Timmy that she could keep a secret too. As they left the pond and headed for the Martin farmhouse, it seemed certain that this summer vacation was sure going to be an especially exciting one for all of them.

2 INDIAN COUNTRY

Uncle Petrie was the one who could tell them something about the find they had made, so Timmy and Boomer went looking for him in the barn. Timmy carried the bucket which contained their treasures.

The old man was almost through with his indoor chores when they came in. He looked at their muddy hands and clothes and asked, "What mischief have you been up to now?"

"Look what we found, Uncle Petrie!" Timmy cried excitedly.

Uncle Petrie came out into the daylight and looked down into the bucket. His eyes lighted up, and he reached in and picked up the broken pottery dish. He examined it carefully.

"Where did you find this?"

"Down in the muskrat village."

The old man laid aside the dish gently, then looked at several of the arrowheads and a spearhead. He coughed. Timmy looked into his old eyes and thought he saw tears there.

"Is there anything wrong, Uncle Petrie?"

Uncle Petrie dabbed at the corners of his eyes with his handkerchief, then shook his head.

"Just memories, Timmy. Makes me think about the Indians I knew when I was about your size."

"Do you think those Indians might have made these things?" Boomer asked, impressed by any man who had known real live Indians.

"I couldn't say for sure," Uncle Petrie replied. Actually he was a little puzzled by the find the boys had made. "Right now I'd say that we would be doing the smart thing if we got our chores done and talked about these relics after supper."

"Relics?" Timmy inquired. "What's 'relics,' Uncle Petrie?"

"Those are things like you have there which tell us a

story about the people who made them many years ago. The more we learn about the arrows and the spears and the dishes, the more we know about the Indians."

"Let's go up to the house and show them to Mom," Timmy urged.

Uncle Petrie took the boy by the arm. "Not yet, we don't. Right now we've got a heap of chores to do. I don't want your mom telling me that I'm spoiling you youngsters. We can have our fun this summer, but we've got to get our work done too."

Timmy looked into the bucket, then up at Uncle Petrie. He just could not understand the old man. Certainly solving this mystery of the Indians was a lot more important than doing chores. Finally he put the bucket inside the barn door and went to feed the chickens and see that there was water in the trough. Boomer helped for a while, then went into the house to call his mother to find out whether he could stay at the Martin farm for supper.

Lassie had her own work to do, and she took care of it proudly. She hurried off to the fields, rounded up the milking cows, and brought them into the barn where Paul and Uncle Petrie would milk them.

As the men were milking the cows, Timmy told his father and Uncle Petrie just how Lassie had uncovered the Indian things.

"Do you think they might have belonged to *your* Indians, Uncle Petrie?" he asked.

"I don't know," Uncle Petrie replied. "They might have been there long before my father came into this country."

"What kind of Indians do you think they were?" Timmy asked. "What could have happened to them?"

"There were a lot of different kinds of Indians," Uncle Petrie told them. "For a while around here we had the Sacs and Foxes, and the Algonquins, and some of the Iroquois tribes came after them. When my father came in here, Indians were coming through all the time. Some of them lived right here in the valley. They did business with the trappers and fur traders who had places where Capitol City is today."

"Gee!" Boomer whistled. "Think of fur traders and trappers in Capitol City." Timmy nodded.

Uncle Petrie carried the milk pail to the separator.

"These Indians and white men got along very well together. The Indians knew where to hunt and trap, and the white men gave them good prices for their skins. My father helped me set up a trap line, and I had a Sac Indian boy who traveled the line with me. He showed me how to skin the animals, and how to dry them on a frame, and other things like that."

"A real Indian?" Boomer inquired.

"A real Indian," Uncle Petrie replied. As they crossed the barnyard to the cream shed, he pointed out Kingpin Mountain about five miles away. "That was once an observation point and sentinel post for the local Indians."

"It would sure make a good one!" Timmy exclaimed. "Anyone up there on the mountain could look up and down the valley for a long ways."

Finally the chores were done. Paul and Uncle Petrie were delighted with the speed and efficiency with which the boys had worked, and Mom was surprised when her "men" arrived early for supper. She steered the boys to the wash basins to clean up. Timmy reluctantly set down his relics, and Lassie took a position over them as though she were guarding them. The collie kept her eyes on the full bowl of food that was awaiting her behind the stove.

Ruth Martin looked from Paul to Uncle Petrie and the boys.

"What's this all about?" she asked. "Seems like a lot of fuss to make over a bucket of fish grubs."

"Oh, it's a lot more than that!" Uncle Petrie assured her. "This time the young'uns have really come up with something. Did you know we had Indians down at the edge of the pond?"

"Indians!" Ruth exclaimed. "When did they move in?"

Timmy and Boomer laughed. Lassie snorted and moved over to her bowl.

"Not now," Timmy said patiently. "A long time ago. We found some of the things they left behind."

Uncle Petrie gave more details while Timmy and Boomer turned to their eating. They reached the pie in good order, then Timmy turned to Uncle Petrie and said, "Now tell us how those things got there, Uncle Petrie. Do you think we might find some more if we kept digging?"

Uncle Petrie raised his hands and shook his head.

"Not yet, not yet," he insisted. "Your mom's had a busy afternoon in the hot kitchen. The least we can do is clean up the dishes and make things neat and tidy for her."

Timmy and Boomer didn't take to this idea happily, but they were so excited about their find that they were willing to pitch in. Lassie looked up and blinked her eyes. She seemed to be pointing out that she had cleaned up her bowl and was glad she knew nothing about washing or drying dishes.

While the boys and Ruth were busy with the dishes, Uncle Petrie collected the Indian curios from the grub bucket and spread them out on a metal tray. He brought them into the living room and set them on the floor. Lassie went with him and sniffed the strange things, trying to decide why they were so important to Timmy.

Then the kitchen brigade came in to join them. Ruth took one look at the relics and said, "So these are the things causing all the excitement! I didn't realize we were in Indian country."

"Oh, yes," Uncle Petrie replied. "Indians lived all over the United States, right out to the Atlantic Ocean."

Timmy nodded in quick agreement. "We read about Pocahontas and Captain John Smith in school," he said. "That was in Virginia."

Boomer smiled. "There were Indians in Massachusetts at the first Thanksgiving too."

"That was Massasoit," Uncle Petrie added. "The Indians were forced to move west as the colonies expanded. Right here in this country we had great herds of bison—the American buffalo. When I was a boy we found buffalo skulls and horns along the streams where the animals came to drink."

Paul turned to Uncle Petrie in surprise. "Are you sure about that buffalo story, Uncle Petrie? I thought buffalo were plains animals."

"Many of them were," Uncle Petrie agreed. "But there's a breed known as the woods buffalo, and there are still large herds of them today up in Canada."

"Uncle Petrie was telling us about Kingpin Mountain," Timmy broke in.

Uncle Petrie smiled at Timmy's excitement. He was talking about a favorite subject.

"You all know the river," he said. "It was one of the main routes of travel for the Indians in their canoes and buffalo-skin boats. The fur trappers and traders used it too. The Indians built birchbark canoes right at the foot of Kingpin Mountain. We call it Kingpin Mountain because it looks like a bowling pin. The Indians called it Sentinel Mountain. It was an observation post where they kept sentinels and scouts all the time."

Paul Martin did not know much about Kingpin Mountain. It was one of the more remote spots in the neighborhood, surrounded by deep woods and in the center of a steep, rocky area. It had been forbidden ground to most of the small boys. But the boy scouts and older youths found it a real delight as a camping and hiking grounds.

"Have you ever been on top of Kingpin Mountain, Uncle Petrie?" Timmy asked.

"A long time ago," Uncle Petrie replied with a touch of pride. "I doubt if my old legs would carry me up there now. I don't reckon it has changed very much, though. Folks just don't go into the woods much now—and very few go mountain climbing."

"I'd sure like to try it," Timmy said quickly.

Uncle Petrie smiled. "When I was your age I knew quite a bit about the woods, and from then on I spent half my time in them. I knew almost as much as the Indians about skinning a deer, building a buffalo-skin boat, setting up a tepee, and making bows and arrows to hunt small game."

Timmy and Boomer looked at Uncle Petrie with new interest. Then Timmy asked, "Did the Indians ride horses in those days?"

"Not around here," Uncle Petrie replied. "The trails were too steep, and many of them were overgrown with brush and vines or blocked by fallen trees."

Timmy was puzzled. "How did they move things from place to place?"

"Long hauls went in their canoes and bullboats on the river," Uncle Petrie explained. "Short hauls were usually carried on the backs of their dogs."

"Dogs?" Timmy and Boomer chorused. "You mean like Lassie?"

Uncle Petrie laughed, rubbed Lassie's forehead, and replied, "I don't suppose many of them were as intelligent or as beautiful as Lassie, but I reckon most of them were as big and strong as she is." Lassie preened herself.

Timmy was curious about this new use for a dog. "What could a dog do?" he asked.

"There were two ways they could be used. One was with a travois made of two poles and a hide between them, with bundles in the hide. The other was with small packs. Something like the leather packs you lads use over the back luggage carrier on your bicycles."

"I'd like to see one of those trav-wah," Boomer broke in.

Paul and Ruth smiled at the seriousness of the boys. But Uncle Petrie was just as serious. He went into the kitchen. While he was gone, Timmy turned to Paul and asked, "What do you think of our Indian things, Dad?"

Paul studied the boy. "I don't know, Timmy. Maybe you've found the key to the Lost Cherokee Treasure!"

"The Lost Cherokee Treasure! What was that?"

Uncle Petrie was back then, carrying two sticks about four feet long and a kitchen towel. He also had a ball of string and a leather belt. He knelt on the carpet.

"Come here, Lassie."

The collie hesitated, looked at Timmy, then decided it was all right to work with Uncle Petrie. The old man adjusted the leather belt about the dog's chest, drew it up until it was reasonably tight, then formed two loops with the string. He attached these to the belt. Next he took one of the sticks and set it in the string loop on Lassie's left side. This went along the dog's flank and touched the floor behind her.

The second stick was fastened on the right side in that same way. Uncle Petrie then looped the towel around the lower end of the two sticks. He picked up several of the spearheads, dropped them into the towel-hammock, and walked across the room.

"Come, Lassie!" he called. The dog came to him, pulling the travois and its cargo behind her.

"That's good," Timmy said happily. "But doesn't it get in her way?"

"Not if it's made right," Uncle Petrie replied. "The sticks must be long enough, so they don't interfere with the movement of the dog's hind legs."

Timmy laughed. "I can make one of those all right," he

said. Then he asked, "Do you know anything about the Lost Cherokee Treasure, Uncle Petrie?"

The older man smiled at Paul, and they both began supplying the story to the boys.

"The Cherokee story isn't a very pleasant one," Uncle Petrie said. "Between 1805 and 1850, when big cities were building on the Atlantic Coast and along the Mississippi River, the United States Government moved the Cherokees and four other tribes to the Indian Territory, which is now Oklahoma."

"I should think the Indians would like that," Timmy said. "It gave them a place of their own, didn't it?"

"Maybe," agreed Uncle Petrie. "But some of the men who moved them were very bad men. The Cherokees were moved out in midwinter in many cases and couldn't take much with them. They called it the Trail of Tears."

Timmy didn't find this very interesting. He turned to Paul and asked, "What about the treasure?"

"One of the legends tells us that the Cherokees had a great treasure when they left the North Carolina mountains. When they arrived in their new homes in eastern Oklahoma it was gone. One of the chiefs explained that thieves tried to steal it from them, and they had to hide it along the trail."

"That's it!" Timmy said excitedly. "These are part of the Lost Cherokee Treasure! It's buried right here on our farm. Boomer and I are going to spend the summer looking for it."

His mother shook her head. "Maybe we ought to get some expert advice about this. Somewhere I read that museums and officials don't like old Indian relics disturbed unless the job is done by experts. Things might be damaged or destroyed."

Timmy looked at Ruth. His face showed his disappointment. Uncle Petrie broke in quickly.

"Let's all sleep on it and talk about it in the morning. Maybe we *will* find that Lost Cherokee Treasure right here on the Martin farm."

The party broke up a few moments later and Paul drove Boomer home. Timmy went to bed with Lassie at the foot of his blankets, but he did not get to sleep for some time. Indians and treasure chests were chasing each other around in his head.

3 ROBBERY AT THE BANK

Timmy was up carly the next morning and rushing around the yard to get his chores done before breakfast. Lassie hurried along behind him. When the cows had been milked, she took them out to the grazing. Then the family gathered about the kitchen table for breakfast.

When no one else brought up the subject, Timmy, bursting with suspense, asked, "What are we going to do about the Indians?"

Ruth and Paul turned to Uncle Petrie as though expecting him to solve the problem.

"We're sure not experts," the older man replied.

Timmy felt as though Uncle Petrie had spoiled things. His pleasant dreams for the summer were being tumbled into dust.

"But couldn't we get some real experts to come out here

and look at the things?" he asked in desperation.

Uncle Petrie looked at Timmy's parents. Ruth studied her son at the other end of the table, then turned to Uncle Petrie and asked, "Do you think there is anyone in town who might help us?"

Uncle Petrie thought for a while. Then he snapped his fingers.

"Not in Calverton, but there is in Capitol City," he declared briskly. "They have a small Indian collection in the public library there. The librarian must be interested in that kind of thing, or she wouldn't keep it. She'll probably know where to get in touch with an expert."

Timmy brightened.

"She should help us," he said quickly. "If she really helped to find the Lost Cherokee Treasure, it would make her famous, wouldn't it?"

"I guess it would," Uncle Petrie agreed.

Ruth turned to Paul. "Well, what about it? Do we help these treasure hunters get to the library?"

"No trouble at all, madam," Paul replied seriously. "Today is my day to go to Capitol City. I've got some business at the Farmers Bank, and the library is right across the street. We'd better rout out Boomer or he'll be disappointed."

Timmy jumped up from the table and ran to the telephone. Lassie followed the boy to show that she wasn't planning on being left out. Arrangements were made to leave a half an hour later.

Uncle Petrie helped to wrap the Indian relics so they would travel without damage. Then Paul brought around the pickup truck just as Boomer came riding into the yard on his bicycle. Mike was not with him. Moments later the passengers for Capitol City were all squeezed into the front seat and Lassie was in the rear of the truck.

Ruth and Uncle Petrie wished them luck.

They talked about the Cherokees and the other Indian tribes all the way to the city. Paul Martin told the boys every Indian story he could remember.

As they came into the main street of Capitol City, their enthusiasm increased but the prospect of the interview with the librarian made the boys quiet. Paul found a parking place close to the library.

"I'll meet you here when you're through," he told Timmy as he collected his papers and started for the bank.

Timmy nodded. He picked up the package of Indian curios carefully, and then with Boomer beside him, he headed for the library. Lassie jumped down from the back of the truck and followed.

Timmy stopped on the library steps. "Sorry, Lassie, but they don't allow dogs in the library. You'll have to wait until we come out."

Lassie hung her head and began pacing up and down the sidewalk as the boys went into the library. Then she jumped back into the pickup truck.

Timmy and Boomer took off their hats as they entered the library and strode up to the main desk. They introduced themselves and told the librarian their story.

Lottie Crane was an understanding woman in her late thirties. She reminded Timmy of his mother. She studied the relics with a good deal of interest and then walked over to the Indian cases and compared some of the items with her own collection.

"I think you've really found something," she told them.

RICAN
INDIAN

"You believe there are other things where you found these?"

"I'm sure of it," Timmy said quickly.

"Why?" asked the librarian.

"Well, like Boomer says, you couldn't have much of an Indian battle with twenty-five arrowheads and a couple of spears."

Lottie Crane laughed pleasantly. Then she pointed to the arrowheads and explained, "I'd say these came from a camp of an Indian who made arrowheads. Some of them aren't finished. The broken dish shows that he cooked and ate there too. I think I'll call your Uncle Petrie on the telephone and talk to him."

Timmy and Boomer were pleased. They felt sure that Uncle Petrie could convince the librarian that the discovery was a big one.

While they waited, they walked over to the window to look out onto the street. It was a warm day and the windows were open. They saw Lassie in the truck, but Paul had not yet finished his business at the bank. As they stood watching, a big black car drew up to a parking place directly in front of the library steps.

Two men climbed out of it, lighted cigarettes, then hurried across the street to the bank. Timmy looked beyond them into the bank through one of the big plate-glass windows to see if he could see his father. Finally he found him near the front of a line at one of the tellers' windows. He would be through in a little while.

Lassie appeared interested in everything going on around her. When the two men moved past the tail gate of the Martin truck, her ruff went up as though she thought they might mean harm to her. She growled in her throat. The men hurried on and went into the bank.

The collie moved to the rear of the truck and put her forepaws up onto the tail gate. Timmy thought the dog was about to leave the truck. He headed for the door of the library, but before he could open it, things began happening across the street.

Through the windows of the bank, the boys saw Paul and the other customers raise their hands above their heads.

"Something's wrong in the bank!" Timmy's shout shattered the silence of the reading room.

Lottie Crane and everyone else reading and studying in the library ran to the windows. Miss Crane took one look and cried, "It's a robbery! Oh, my, oh, my! I hope no one is hurt."

She ran back to her desk to call the police and the sheriff's office. Timmy turned to Boomer, his face very white.

"Do you think they'll hurt my dad?"

"I don't know," Boomer replied helplessly. "You can't tell what a man with a gun is going to do. But—but I don't think they'll hurt anybody."

"I hope not."

At the thought of any harm coming to Paul, Timmy could not stand still any longer. He opened the door and stepped outside.

Across the street he could see two men in the bank working along as though the whole job had been carefully planned. One of the robbers stood near the door of the bank, holding his gun on the armed bank guard and keeping the customers in line.

The other held his weapon pointed at the bank employees and accepted the money that was pushed across the marble counter in his direction.

As Timmy watched, two women fainted and dropped to the floor of the bank. His father knelt down to help one of them. The robber nearest him said something and pointed the pistol right at Paul's head.

"No, no!" Timmy cried, although it was obvious that the man in the bank could not hear him. He ran toward their truck where Lassie was jumping up and down at the sight of him. The collie apparently sensed that something was wrong inside the bank.

The robber with the money was stuffing it into two large canvas bags. When they were full, he backed toward the door. Timmy heard the library doors open and close behind him, and when he turned to look back he saw Boomer and Miss Crane standing at the top of the steps. Miss Crane was holding her fist to her mouth and calling, "Where are the police? Where is the sheriff? Why don't they get here!"

Several men started converging on the bank. By this time, however, the bank robbers were out of the bank doorway. One of them took the two money sacks and, staggering under their weight, hurried across the street while the other one held the two guns and threatened the people around him.

Timmy realized that they were going to get away. They were thieves, and what was worse, the running man had threatened his father. When Paul had dropped to the floor to help the woman who had fainted, he had disappeared from Timmy's sight. He might have been hurt in there. Timmy turned toward the truck.

"Lassie! Lassie, get him! Go after him, Lassie!"

Lassie did not need any more urging. She darted out into the street as the bank robber ran for the car. She tripped him, and he fell heavily to the ground. Another man jumped out of the getaway car, grabbed up the money-bags which fell from the hands of Lassie's victim, and cried, "Get rid of that dog!"

As he flung the money into the automobile, he kicked at Lassie's shoulder and threw her off balance. But his own escape was uppermost in his mind. He climbed back into the driver's seat.

Lassie realized that the first man, on his hands and

knees in the street, was stunned and no longer a menace. She turned at once to the man with the guns who was climbing into the back seat of the car. Even the fact that he was already in the getaway car did not stop the brave dog. She went after him, leaping into the rear seat where he crouched.

"Get going, get going!" the robber shouted as he wrestled with the powerful dog. "Let's get out of here!"

The big car roared and took off down the street, tires squealing. Timmy was stunned as he saw Lassie disappear into the getaway car. He cried out but no one heard him, for things were in a turmoil on the main street of Capitol City. Sirens began screaming toward the bank from all directions. The bank's burglar alarm was wailing. Patrolmen came running from around the corner, pulling at their holsters to get out their guns.

"Lassie, Lassie!" Timmy shouted above the uproar. "Come back, Lassie!"

But his cries were useless. The getaway car headed away as fast as it could go. The bandits had just cleared the nearest intersection when the first policeman came on the run. He recognized the situation and fired several shots after the fleeing auto.

Timmy covered his eyes.

"Don't shoot Lassie! Don't shoot my dog!"

No one could hear him.

Police cars and Sheriff Casey's station wagon were coming around the corner now. The officers jumped out and began asking questions. People were milling around, getting in each other's way and improving the chances of the bank robbers' escape.

Timmy stared down the street, his eyes full of tears. He bit his lips as he turned to Boomer.

"Do you think they'll hurt her?"

Boomer didn't know what to say. He had heard one of the robbers order Lassie shot, just as Timmy had. But it might have been an empty threat. The two boys were left alone with their grief as the librarian, the townspeople, and the police officers all converged on the fallen bank robber in the middle of the street. Several of the townspeople wanted to beat him up, but the officers took him into custody promptly.

Timmy gripped Boomer by the arm. "We'd better go find my dad and see if he's all right."

They hurried across the street toward the bank. As they came up on the sidewalk, several of the local traffic police were trying to calm the crowd. Timmy and Boomer pushed past them and were almost at the door of the bank when they spied Paul. He was talking to the woman he had helped during the robbery. He was holding a handkerchief with smelling salts under her nose.

"Are you all right, Dad?" Timmy asked, grasping Paul by the hand.

"I'm all right, son."

Timmy's voice broke. "Lassie's gone! They've taken her away."

Paul put an arm around Timmy, then tightened his grip on the shaking boy.

"I saw part of it, son," he said. "We'll do everything we can to get her back. You can depend on that!"

Timmy hid his face in his father's jacket as one of the town constables came up and said, "Mr. Martin, that was sure a good job your dog did there."

Paul nodded. Some of the people around him shook their heads. There was moisture in the eyes of some of the women. They looked at Timmy soberly, as though they were thinking that this might be the last good job that Lassie would ever do.

"What—what do you think they'll do to her?" Timmy choked on the words.

"I don't think they'll do anything to her," Paul tried to reassure him. "As long as we're holding one of them a prisoner, the others won't want to make the situation any worse than it is. I think Lassie will be all right."

Timmy relaxed a bit. A lot of grown-up business was going on around him and Boomer, and they didn't understand what it was all about. Constable Frank Dillon was explaining his actions to Paul Martin and the boys knew Paul would tell them about it later, on the way home.

"These robbers are in for a heap of trouble," Dillon said. "Robbing a bank ain't as easy to get away with as it used to be. I've already notified Sheriff Bert Casey, and he'll have his patrols out along all the highways right away. These men can't get very far. Bob Hanson, the banker, is in touch with the Federal authorities, and they'll be moving in here before we know it. Nobody can buck that kind of a combination and get away with it."

Paul realized that the officials would be doing everything they could. But as he watched Timmy he knew that all of this would not ease the mind of the boy as far as his dog was concerned. The best thing was to try to think about something else for a little while.

"What did the librarian say about the Indian things?" he asked Timmy.

Timmy looked at his father for some moments as though he could not believe his ears. Then he shook his head slowly and said, "Nothing."

Paul turned to Boomer, who shrugged.

"She seemed to like the things, and she still has them in there. She was going to call up Uncle Petrie and talk to him."

"I think I'll go in and talk to her. Do you fellows want to come along?" Paul asked.

Timmy bit his lip and looked at Boomer. They followed Paul into the library.

While her human friends worried, Lassie was going through an experience that was new and frightening. As soon as the getaway car was out of town, the driver asked tensely, "Do you think Jack will keep mum?"

The man in the back seat did not answer, and the driver realized that his companion was still having a rough time with Lassie.

"Shall I stop and push her out?" he demanded.

"No, no!" cried the bandit. "Keep driving! Didn't you hear those sirens? If we don't keep going, we'll have trouble in big doses. I'll handle the dog!"

The driver turned back to his job, and Lassie and her enemy fought in the confined space of the back seat. Finally the robber rolled over on the collie and pinned her down in spite of all her efforts to throw him off. She snapped and snarled, but the bandit held her jaws together in an iron grip.

Much of Lassie's wisdom lay in the fact that she knew the time to fight and the time to wait. A better opportunity might come to her later on. Apparently giving up, she relaxed on the floor of the car, and the bank robber

pushed himself up on the seat. He kept a foot on the collie's neck and tried to brush himself off.

"That's better," he commented.

The driver nodded, then repeated, "What about Jack?"

"Jack is a pretty smart boy. He'll sit tight and wait for us to try some way to get him out of jail. And even if we can't spring him, I think he'll feel that one third of eighty thousand dollars is worth a few years in jail. Who knows?" The man grinned. "We could probably do something about that too. I've cased this whole deal, and that prison in Capitol City is a cinch to crack when the time comes. But right now we've got to keep away from all kinds of cops."

"Where do we head from here, Bill?" the driver continued.

"Just like I told you," Bill Gates replied. "The sheriff and the highway patrol will be blocking the main highways. But I don't figure they'll be smart enough to figure we might show up on the other side of Kingpin Mountain. You head up that dirt road I showed you. We'll hide the money and then hike out across the mountain to where we left the other car—just the way we planned."

Sam Rowan nodded.

"You're sure smart, Bill. I hear tell that even the local folks don't cross this Kingpin Mountain. It's mighty wild country from what little I've seen of it. Are you sure you can find the way?"

"I can find the way, all right," Gates assured him.

"Okay, okay." Rowan found the dirt road and turned onto it.

Lassie sat up and looked out of the window, as though trying to remember just where they were going. Her movement reminded Rowan of her presence.

"What are we going to do with the dog?"

Bill Gates snorted. "I wanted to finish her off when she barged into the car, but you wouldn't have anything to do with it."

Sam Rowan shook his head and shuddered. "I don't go for killing. Not even dogs."

"Some day you may have to kill. Then what are you going to do?"

"I don't ever want to see that day," Rowan declared

fervently. And he did not waver during the argument that followed.

Finally Bill Gates shook his head. "We'll leave the dog in the car when we take off into the woods," he agreed.

Rowan relaxed and kept driving along the bumpy dirt road. Lassie seemed to sense something of the thoughts in Bill Gates's mind. A low growl formed in her throat, but when Gates prodded her with his knee, she settled down and remained quiet.

Finally the road narrowed down to little more than a trail and ended in a clump of bushes. Rowan braked the car to a stop, then climbed out and stretched his legs. Gates held Lassie by the collar with one hand and passed one of the heavy currency bags to his partner with the other.

"Take this," he said. "Go around those bushes to your right and you'll find a trail that goes right up Kingpin Mountain. I'll catch up to you in a few minutes. I want to brush out the trail."

Rowan shouldered the bag of money, found the path without any trouble, and started climbing. Gates threw the other moneybag out onto the ground, then pushed Lassie back into the far corner of the rear seat and slammed the door.

Lassie was off balance for a moment, but when she recovered she flung herself across the cushion toward her tormentor. Bill Gates merely laughed. Moving swiftly, he opened the front door on the driver's side of the car, reached in, and released the hand brake. Lassie leaped into the front seat, aiming for the bandit's arm, but he was too quick for her.

He slammed the front door. Then he threw his weight against the car and the heavy auto started moving forward. It broke through the bushes ahead of it and rolled down a small slope.

When the bushes were pushed aside, it could be seen that the dirt road had once led to the edge of a stone quarry. The big hole in the ground was only about fifty feet beyond the car, and it was filled with water.

Lassie saw the trap which was ahead for her, but it did not look as though there was anything she could do about it. A loud laugh came from Bill Gates as he turned to pick up the bag of money and followed his partner.

Then the front wheels of the car came to the edge of the quarry; the heavy machine dropped down onto the frame and slid forward with a loud crash. When the rear wheels caught on the lip of the pit, the car turned over in midair and dropped into the water.

Lassie was barking loudly, but there was no one there to hear.

4 TRAIL OF THE CHEROKEE

The talk with Lottie Crane showed Timmy and his companions that she was greatly interested in the Indian discoveries. But just what she could do about the expert was something she would have to check. She assured the boys and Paul Martin that she would let them know as soon as she had something to report.

Paul nodded. Then, for the ears of the librarian alone, he said, "If it's good news, I hope Timmy hears it quick. If anything has happened to Lassie, Timmy will need a lot of good news to make up for that."

The sheriff had arrived at the scene of the robbery when they came back to the truck. Paul joined a number of other Capitol City folks who were asking questions about the chase. Sheriff Bert Casey, a tall, determined-looking fellow, didn't say much to most of the people, but when Paul

Martin came up, he took him by the arm and said, "I'd like to talk to you, Paul."

"Sure thing, Bert."

"What's this I hear about the dog?"

Paul looked toward the drooping Timmy and Boomer in the front seat of the truck. Then he replied, "She delivered one of the robbers for you. But I guess they're going to have a chance to get even with her, any way they see fit."

"I wouldn't say that," Sheriff Casey declared. "That collie of yours has been in on a lot of excitement around this country, and she usually comes through with flying colors. I'd make a bet she's going to be the one to bring in the rest of those bandits."

"I hope you're right," Paul said. "But I'm sure wondering what I'm going to tell Ruth when we get back to the farm. She'll blame me for losing Lassie!"

Bert Casey slapped the farmer on the shoulder. "My money's still on Lassie. We'll keep a sharp eye out for her, and if she does show up at your place, you give us a call this evening."

"Thanks, Sheriff."

Paul walked around to the driver's side of the truck, climbed in, and started the motor. Timmy and Boomer studied him for some moments and then Timmy asked, "What did Sheriff Casey say about Lassie?"

His father chuckled. "He thinks Lassie is bright enough to bring in those two bank robbers singlehanded."

"Doesn't he think they'll hurt her?"

"Not our Lassie," Paul assured him. "He's sure she's going to be all right."

Timmy and Boomer were silent as they headed back to Calverton, then drove up the road that led to the Bates and Martin farms. Paul stopped at Boomer's house and Mike came dashing out to greet them. The sight of the little dog, alive and well, brought a lump into Timmy's throat and he fought back the tears that came into his eyes.

Boomer knew just how Timmy was feeling. "Don't worry, Timmy," he said as he climbed down from the truck. "Lassie is going to be all right. I'm sure of it."

"Good-by, Boomer," Paul called. "I'll bring your bike over tonight. We'll let you know if anything comes up about the Indian business or the bank robbery."

"Thank you, Mr. Martin," Boomer replied. Then he walked slowly toward the front door of his house.

It didn't take long to reach the Martin farm. But the house was closed up and quiet. Paul drove around to the garage and put the truck away. Then he took Timmy by the hand and they walked across to the kitchen door. "Ruth! Ruth!" Paul called. "Uncle Petrie!"

There was no answer. They went into the kitchen and looked all around. There was a half-finished meal on the table. Pans still stood on the stove. It looked as though Ruth had been called away in a hurry.

"Where's Mom?" Timmy quavered. "Is she gone too?"

Paul Martin paled. The farm was the last one out on the road that led to one side of Kingpin Mountain. There was a chance that the bank robbers had taken this route and had kidnaped Ruth as well as the collie.

Timmy sat down at the kitchen table. He felt like crying, but spending so much time with his father and Uncle Petrie had given him a grown-up attitude toward many things. He waited quietly while Paul went through the house looking for a note from Ruth or anything else that might tell him where she had gone.

Timmy had been alone in the kitchen only a couple of minutes when the door banged open and his mother rushed in.

"Timmy! Timmy!" she cried. "Are you all right?"

"I'm all right," Timmy said. "We were worried about you!"

"Where's Dad? Is he all right?"

"He's upstairs, looking for you," Timmy replied. Then he clung to his mother. "Mommy, Mommy!" he whispered. "It's Lassie—she's gone—maybe for good!"

"Don't worry about Lassie," Ruth calmed him. "She's one lady in this house who always seems to be able to take care of herself, no matter what happens."

Paul heard the conversation in the kitchen and came hurrying down.

"Where have you been?" he demanded. "What have you been doing?"

Timmy shivered at the sharpness of the tone. But Ruth smiled and said calmly, "Don't get excited, dear. It's so wonderful to see you both alive and well. I thought you were in big trouble. What in the world happened?"

"It was a bank robbery," Paul explained. "Three men held up the Capitol City Farmers Bank and got away with about eighty thousand dollars. I was in the bank when two of them came in with pistols and robbed the tellers. The third one waited in the getaway car. Your son was something of a hero," Paul concluded, to lighten some of the tension.

"Timmy?" Ruth said. "Timmy—mixed up in the bank robbery?"

"In a way," Paul replied. "But I don't think any of them saw him, or even knew he was there. When he saw the bank robbers coming out of the bank, he sent Lassie after them. Our old girl went right after those two bandits as though she was chasing Timmy's beach ball. She knocked one of them down in the middle of Main Street and followed the other one right into the getaway car. . . ." Timmy gulped. His father turned and looked out the window.

"Lassie's gone," Timmy insisted. "And she's never coming back. I know it, I know it!"

Ruth Martin hugged him then, and said, "I think we're getting excited over nothing! I've been worried about you —you've been worried about me—and we've all been worried about Lassie. Let's go out to the barn and see what we find there!"

Ruth led the way to the barn at a fast walk. Her "men" came along behind her. As they came into the semidarkness of the big building, they could hear Uncle Petrie's voice saying, "Now take it easy, girl. None of these brambles and buckthorns are going to kill you. Not a courageous female like you, no sirree!"

Timmy came to a full stop. He heard a mewling sound that he recognized as a protest from his collie.

"Lassie! Lassie! Oh, Lassie!"

He ran forward to where Uncle Petrie was kneeling beside the big dog.

Lassie was a sight. Instead of the clean, shiny coat she had worn when she was getting ready for the trip to Capitol City, her brown and white fur was spotted with brambles, matted with mud, and dripping with water.

"She sure looks as though she's been running wild in the

woods," Uncle Petrie declared. "Where did you fellows turn her loose? You had Ruth plumb scared. She thought the truck had run off the road, and you menfolks had been busted up. She figured Lassie came home to tell us you were in some kind of trouble. But we didn't know where to begin looking for you."

Paul Martin laughed in genuine relief. "It wasn't us, Uncle Petrie. It was those bank robbers who kidnaped Lassie!"

"Bank robbers!" Uncle Petrie snorted. "Kidnaped Lassie?" He looked from Paul to Timmy. "What bank robbers? Why did they kidnap Lassie? Was anyone hurt? How much did they get away with? Oh, golly, I knew I should have gone along with you!"

Timmy and his dad smiled as they saw Uncle Petrie's excitement building up. Suddenly the old man turned to Timmy and dropped a hand on his shoulder. "They didn't do anything to those Indian curios of yours, did they?"

"Oh, no," Timmy replied. "The Indian things were safe in the library before the bank robbery started."

Ruth was gripping Paul by the arm and looking up at

him as if he might have been a special target of the bank robbers.

"Were you—were you in the bank when it happened?"

"I was there, all right," Paul told her softly. "Let's get Lassie cleaned up, and then we'll talk about it."

Timmy and Uncle Petrie set to work while Timmy told about the bank robbery and Lassie's part in it. His uncle listened and tried to calm him down.

When Lassie was finally presentable, she climbed to her feet, nuzzled the three adults gently, then took her place alongside Timmy. They went outside, followed by Paul and Ruth, who headed for the kitchen. Uncle Petrie joined the family after he had put the cleaning things away.

"Lassie looks as though she wants to go back into the woods," Timmy said, as they stood looking up at the drifting clouds.

"No sirree!" Uncle Petrie insisted. "Not after all the trouble we've had cleaning her up from the last time. We'll tie her up in the barn, if need be. No more woods-romping tonight."

"Do you think she might know something about where

those bank robbers are hiding out?" Timmy asked suddenly.

Uncle Petrie considered this question for a while, then shook his head.

"Those bank robbers are desperate men. They're not going to wait around for a dog to lead the police to them. If they figured Lassie was going to make any trouble for them, they'd have killed her, sure enough. The fact that she's come home is a sure sign they're a long ways from here."

5 A HIKE ON KINGPIN MOUNTAIN

Timmy was a different boy that night, with Lassie safely home again. The threat of the bank robbers had been pushed to the back of his mind. When Ruth asked for details of the librarian's talk with him about the Indian relics, he said, "She liked them! She said that she had brought her Indian collection with her when she came to Capitol City. She'd never heard of Indians living in this part of the country. But when I told her about the Cherokees passing through on their way to Oklahoma, she knew about them and their Trail of Tears. She said that we had probably found a camp of some arrowhead makers—because some of the flint arrowheads were only partly finished."

"Did she say she could help you find an expert?"

The boy shook his head, then turned to Uncle Petrie.

"Didn't she talk to you on the telephone?"

"Oh, yes," Uncle Petrie replied with a smile. "She was glad that I sent you to see her. She said she had some friends in Washington at the Smithsonian Institution. They're very much interested in the American Indian. Some of our best Indian experts come from there. She said if this was a clue to the whereabouts of the Lost Cherokee Treasure, they would consider it a find of utmost importance."

Timmy frowned and asked, "What's 'utmost'?"

His father smiled. "That means it is one of the biggest things that could happen."

Timmy puffed up like a pouter pigeon. Then he frowned again and turned to Uncle Petrie.

"Did she say anything about Boomer and me working with the expert if he does come out here?"

"I don't think she mentioned that," Uncle Petrie replied. "But someone has to show him the places where the Indians lived and worked. It might as well be you and Boomer."

"Maybe they'd rather have you," Timmy suggested reluctantly.

Uncle Petrie made a face. He rubbed his back and his legs as though they were not as strong as they had been. "Like I told you, I'm not much of a hiker any more. I reckon I've got the gumption to make one good climb up Kingpin Mountain, and that would be the end of it."

"Maybe one good climb would be enough for the Indian expert," Timmy pointed out.

Uncle Petrie smiled. Then with a wink in the direction of Ruth and Paul, he said, "If this expert wants to go along with me, he'll have to be showing up here bright and early in the morning, 'cause that's when I'm going to take you and Boomer to Sentinel Rock. We'll make a map as we go along. From then on, you and Boomer will have to worry about your Indian expert. I'll be taking it easy in the hammock and looking at the mountain from this end of the trail."

Timmy smiled. This would make it a lot easier to convince the Indian authority that the boys could serve him as the best possible helpers.

When dinner was finished, Paul Martin went to the telephone and lifted the receiver. After grinding the bell, he said, "Hello, Jenny, put me through to Sheriff Casey in Capitol City."

Jenny started to make the connection, and as she did she asked, "Heard anything from Lassie?"

"Yes!" Paul replied. "That's the news I want to pass along. Lassie's home."

"Oh, I'm so glad to hear that," replied the telephone operator.

Sheriff Casey came on the wire then, and Paul told him about Lassie's return.

"Any clues that might lead us to those bank robbers?" Casey inquired quickly.

"Nothing you could hang anything onto," Paul declared. "She was sure messed up, as if they had turned her loose in the woods. But they didn't hurt her—I was a little surprised at that."

"I'll have a posse combing those woods around your place as soon as I can round one up," Casey said. "We haven't had any luck anywhere else. The car hasn't come up to any of the roadblocks, and none of the police search parties have come up with anything."

"How about the one you caught?"

"He's as mum as a stone idol. Won't even give us his right name. We're trying to check his record by fingerprints and photo files, but so far there's nothing doing. I'll keep in touch with you if anything does come up. Maybe that dog of yours can be a big help to us before this is over."

Paul talked for a while longer, then hung up and returned to his family. He shook his head.

"The sheriff has no news about the bank robbers. He seems pretty sure that they're still in the area, but he doesn't know exactly where."

"Do you think they might be hiding on Kingpin Mountain?" Timmy asked.

"If they are, then they're trapped," Paul pointed out. "There are only two roads leading to Kingpin Mountain—one on this side from Calverton and the other on the north side from Lewiston. The sheriff will certainly have them blocked."

Timmy's chief interest in the whereabouts of the robbers was based on his worry about how they might interfere with the search for the Indian relics and the solving of the Cherokee Indian mystery. He looked up quickly when Ruth took Paul by the arm and asked, "If the robbers are on Kingpin Mountain, do you think it's safe for Uncle Petrie and the boys to go up there tomorrow?"

Paul studied his son and Uncle Petrie.

"I spoke to the sheriff about that. He believes it's safe if they stay on the main trails. In fact he seemed to think that if the bank bandits did see Uncle Petrie and the boys on the mountain, they might try to break out, and he'd be ready for them."

Ruth put an arm about Timmy. "In that case, dear, you'd better be heading for bed. Tomorrow will be a very busy day."

Timmy needed no urging to get him off to bed early, and Lassie went along dutifully.

Early the next morning Boomer and Mike arrived. The Bates boy had received permission to go on the hike up Kingpin Mountain, and his dog looked as eager as his master. Lassie's interest appeared to be divided. She sensed that they were going somewhere, but until they started it would be impossible to tell whether or not it was where she wanted to go.

Uncle Petrie and the boys carried knapsacks with ample food supplies in them. Lassie and Mike remained close to Timmy and Boomer, depending upon them for a share of the rations.

Paul and Ruth waved good-by, and the party headed out on the trail. Timmy set the pace because he was the smallest. As he strode along on one side of Uncle Petrie he asked, "Where are we going first?"

"I've got several places in mind," Uncle Petrie replied. "First we'll start up along the river, and I'll show you where the Indians built their canoes and bullboats."

"What's a bullboat?" Timmy asked. "You said something about that the other night."

"A bullboat was a round boat which the Indians made by tying half a dozen sticks together to form a frame. Then they stretched a buffalo bull's hide over it to make the outside covering. It was a lot better than other boats for riding in rough water, and along rapids and places of that kind. It wouldn't get stuck on the rocks, and it would ride over a lot of shallow water without piling up like a canoe would do. It was almost impossible to turn it over in the water."

Uncle Petrie turned into the trail that led down to the river's edge. But Lassie was holding back, and it looked as though she had her own ideas about where she wanted to go. She kept breaking away into the woods for several minutes at a time, barking and then running back to join the others. Mike followed her on several occasions but found nothing that interested him.

Finally Uncle Petrie faced the collie and said sternly, "If you don't want to come with us, Lassie, you can go home!"

Timmy knelt alongside his dog and held her around the neck. "Don't you want us to know about the Indian places?" he whispered.

Lassie whimpered. Timmy laid his head on her shoulder and rubbed his ear against her mane. Then he jumped up.

"Come on, Lassie, we're losing time. It'll be after dark before we get up the mountain and back down again."

They stopped for a while at the bullboat bay. Uncle

Petrie cut some of the willow wands and showed the boys how they would bend and shape themselves into frames for the boats.

"We'll leave them here to dry," he said finally, "and maybe we can come back some day and finish a boat if we can find the right kind of hide."

Timmy and Boomer both thought this was a splendid idea.

Uncle Petrie then showed them a grove of large birch trees where the Indians had cut the bark and formed it into the coverings for their birchbark canoes.

"If this Indian expert does a mite of digging around here, he might find ax heads and adz stones that were used for trimming these canoes," Uncle Petrie continued.

Timmy and Boomer wanted to try a little digging right then and there. But Uncle Petrie reminded them, "No more digging until the expert is here to tell us how it should be done. We'll be heading up the mountain now. And we'd better start making that map we've been talking about."

A good part of the morning had passed and the three

were hungry. It did not take much prodding from Boomer to get Uncle Petrie and Timmy to agree to stop a little longer and eat their lunch.

While they were eating and throwing tidbits to the dogs, Uncle Petrie took out a heavy piece of paper and some pencils. He opened up his compass and then spread out a town map of Calverton which included Kingpin Mountain and the surrounding country. He pointed to an indicator on his town map.

"That's what the map-makers call a rose. Sometimes it really looks like a rose, particularly on a marine map for ships on rivers or on the oceans. Sometimes it's just an arrow with a pair of crossbars like a television aerial on the roof."

"What's it for?" Timmy asked.

"The top of the rose or the point of the arrow will be showing you the North Star," Uncle Petrie explained. "In that way you can make sure that the places on your map are in the right positions."

"Oh, I've seen that in the cub scout handbook," Boomer broke in. "My father says it goes back to the time when sea captains like Columbus or Magellan liked to decorate their charts and log books."

"That's right," Uncle Petrie agreed. "But a map can tell more than directions. When a man like our Indian expert looks at a map of a mountain, he wants to know a lot of things folks in town would know. He wants to know where the trees are, where the rocks are, and whether there are any hills running up on either side of Kingpin Mountain."

Timmy was puzzled. "How can you show that on a map?"

"There are ways," Uncle Petrie said. He took a pencil and drew a series of O's linked together in a circle. "That's the mark on a map for trees." Then he wrote down a number of U's in a line, connected them with upside-down U's, and asked, "What does this look like?"

Timmy studied it for a while. "It looks like a broken chain."

"Good!" Uncle Petrie exclaimed. "It is a chain—a chain of hills or mountains."

Timmy was interested and curious. He looked at the

marks, then asked, "How do you know whether it's a hill or a mountain?"

"That's easy," Uncle Petrie replied. "If you're drawing a map of a low hill, you draw lines around it every hundred feet as you go toward the top. You mark these *100, 200, 300, 400,* and so forth, at the levels. If it's a mountain, you'd have something above a thousand feet, so each one of the lines would be marked in thousand-foot levels."

"Golly," laughed Timmy, "that sure makes a map tell you things, doesn't it?"

"It sure does," Uncle Petrie agreed. Then he drew a group of sample markings that represented sand, rock, and other materials on one margin of the map, so the boys could copy them as they were needed.

"This is the river," he explained, as he marked in the bullboat camp and the birch grove in which they were sitting. He sketched out the trail up to Sentinel Rock and said, "We'll mark in the details as we come to them."

This gave the boys something new to think about as they continued on their hike. Boomer called out some of the sights for the map, and Timmy marked them down. Once or twice Boomer asked to hold the map, but he didn't really enjoy adding the tiny marks to the drawing. As a result, he soon lost interest in the map-making.

Timmy kept on. He was determined to have all the information handy if the Indian expert asked him about the different Cherokee camping sites on Kingpin Mountain.

When they were still about a mile from Sentinel Rock, Boomer stumbled over a rock, tripped, and fell. Timmy and Uncle Petrie ran to help him up. They examined his leg and Uncle Petrie washed it with a sterile solution and cleaned the bleeding cut.

"Are you tired, Boomer?" he asked.

"I guess I am."

"Tired?" Timmy inquired with a frown. "Or just tired of hiking?"

Uncle Petrie patted Timmy on the shoulder. "If Boomer wants to rest, we'll be glad to have him rest. This is a pretty rugged mountain. It wasn't built for small boys."

Timmy and Boomer laughed. Timmy realized that he was getting tired too, but his excitement over the coming of the Indian expert was enough to send him along the rest of the way with Uncle Petrie.

"I reckon I'll stay here and rest for a while," Boomer declared. "You can pick me up on your way back. I can see about all I want to see from here. And if the expert does let us come along to work with him, I'll know as much about it as I want to know."

Uncle Petrie agreed. He and Timmy continued their climb. Lassie had caught something of the spirit of the hike and was running and leaping and barking beside them.

They reached Sentinel Rock and Timmy was thrilled. He stood on the same spot where the Indian sentries had stood and looked out over the valley. Uncle Petrie was tired out, however, and he began to wonder whether he hadn't taken on a job that would be too much for him.

He pointed out the Martin farm far down below the rock; then he showed Timmy the locations of the camps on the river which they had visited. Timmy worked on his map, making notes carefully and listening to everything Uncle Petrie said.

Finally the old man pointed along the trail about half a mile ahead of them. "The Indian caves are up there. The tribes and bands who set up the lookouts here usually lived there when they camped on Kingpin Mountain. You'll be able to find it from here without any trouble. I'll round out your map for you when we get back to the farm."

The day had been a full one, and man and boy were more than ready to turn back. Lassie acted as though she didn't care one way or another. She found many things in the woods to interest her.

Timmy called the collie and they started down the mountain. Twilight was closing in about them, and Uncle Petrie said, "I'm glad we have our flashlights. If we're not careful we'll have to use your map to find our way home."

"Lassie knows the way," Timmy replied. "We'll never be lost while we have her along."

Lassie barked to accept the compliment. Then she bounded along the return trail ahead of them. Everything went smoothly until they came to the point where they had left Boomer. The Bates boy was nowhere in sight.

Timmy pointed to a rock beside the path. "We left him right there, didn't we?"

Uncle Petrie nodded. "That's the place, all right."

It was getting darker by the minute. Timmy cupped his hand over his mouth and called, "Boomer, Boomer! Where are you?"

They listened for a moment. Then a weird voice replied, "Boomer! Boomer! Where are you?"

Timmy shivered. He gripped Uncle Petrie's arm.

"It's just an echo," the old man explained. "But Boomer should certainly have heard us if he's anywhere around. That echo must have come from the cliffs on the other side of the river valley."

"Are there any real wild animals on this mountain?" Timmy asked nervously.

Uncle Petrie bit his lip. He realized the thoughts that were going through Timmy's mind.

"Some," he replied reluctantly.

"Dad once said something about bears and mountain lions," Timmy remembered.

"I reckon they're both up here," Uncle Petrie agreed. "But I wouldn't worry too much about them. There's plenty of game around for the lions, and plenty of berries for the bears, so they wouldn't bother humans."

Timmy nodded, obviously not convinced. Then, as usual, he turned to his collie. He roughed up her coat, patted her on the shoulder, and said, "Lassie, go find Boomer!"

The collie moved over to the smooth stone with Timmy. She sniffed around for a while, then started off into the woods beyond the small clearing.

6 THE INDIAN EXPERT

As soon as they saw which way Lassie was going, Timmy and Uncle Petrie turned on their flashlights and followed her. The darkness brought out strange sounds in the night. Timmy was afraid, but he didn't want anyone to know that. He kept close to Uncle Petrie, actually brushing against him now and then.

"What's that?" he kept asking.

Uncle Petrie stopped and listened. "It's small animals in the grass. They know Lassie is here and they don't want her to find them."

Suddenly there was a stirring in the trees over their heads. Timmy came to a full stop. He looked up and shone his flashlight into the branches. Two bright yellow and green eyes looked down at him. There was a whirring sound like a large airplane propeller, and Timmy shouted, "Run,

Uncle Petrie! Come on, run!"

Instead of running, Uncle Petrie came to a full stop and laughed.

A reply came from the tree. "Who—ooo to—whooo!"

"It's nothing but a great horned owl," Uncle Petrie explained. "He's waiting for us to get out of his way, so he can go hunting for some of those field mice we've been stirring up."

"I sure hope we find Boomer soon," Timmy said. "I don't want to be out here in these big woods any longer than we have to. Do you think he's hurt?"

"I hope not," Uncle Petrie replied. "Say, Lassie sounds as though she's found something."

Timmy listened and realized that Lassie was barking the short barks which usually signaled a victory. They hurried along and finally met the collie on the trail.

Timmy took her by the collar and moved ahead with her, while Uncle Petrie came along more slowly.

The boy and the dog came into a small clearing. Half-way across there was a rotting log, and sprawled across it was Boomer Bates. Timmy slid to a halt, turned his flashlight on Boomer's dirty clothes, and then ran the light over the boy's hands and face.

"Uncle Petrie!" he cried. "Uncle Petrie! Here he is—and he's all covered with blood!"

Uncle Petrie hurried across the clearing and halted beside Timmy. Lassie was the only one who knew what to do. She went over to Boomer and began licking the boy's face. Soon he opened his eyes and looked around him.

Uncle Petrie relaxed. "Boomer's all right, Timmy," he said. "That isn't blood. That's berry juice. I guess Boomer got a little hungry and went to look for something to eat."

A sigh of relief came from Timmy. Boomer looked up and rubbed his eyes.

"I was tired," he said simply. "I guess I fell asleep."

Uncle Petrie nodded. "Everything's all right, now that we're together again. We'd better hurry along home. The folks will be worrying about us."

Lassie led the way back toward the downhill trail, and the walking was much easier.

"Did you see anyone in the woods?" Boomer asked.

Timmy shook his head slowly. "No, why?"

"I heard all kinds of sounds," Boomer declared, "and I thought I saw lights and fires and things."

"The sounds were probably field mice or raccoons or opossum," Timmy replied sagely.

"Or great horned owls," Uncle Petrie reminded him with a chuckle.

Boomer's words did alert both Timmy and Uncle Petrie, however. As they walked along they looked around them in the woods. Suddenly Timmy said, "Look way over there, Uncle Petrie. Isn't that a campfire? Do you think someone might be out looking for us?"

"More likely it's one of the sheriff's posses out looking for the bank bandits," Uncle Petrie reminded them.

Boomer grabbed Timmy's arm. "Or it could be the bank robbers themselves!" he cried.

"We're not going to look for either one," Uncle Petrie said firmly. "Let's keep moving."

As they came down the hill, they lost the trail two or three times. Each time Timmy turned to the collie and shouted, "Home, Lassie, take us home!"

And each time the dog checked the darkness around

them, then barked happily and picked up the right route. The tired boys and their older guardian tagged along quickly.

Finally a light in the Martin window could be seen.

"That's it!" Timmy shouted. "We're almost there."

Lassie began barking. The kitchen door opened and Ruth Martin called, "Timmy! Uncle Petrie! Is that you?"

"It's us, all right. Boy, are we glad to be home! But we sure had an exciting day," Timmy replied happily.

Paul came up behind Ruth. "I'm glad to hear that. I was just about to call the sheriff and ask him to help us look for you."

"I'm sorry we're late," Uncle Petrie said. "Boomer had a little trouble, and we had something of a job helping him out of it."

Boomer looked at the ground. Ruth and Paul were wise enough not to ask any questions.

"I've got some warm supper on the stove," Ruth said. "We'll look after that, then we can take Boomer home."

"That's my job," Uncle Petrie insisted. "But a nice hot meal would make things look a lot brighter. Eh, Timmy?"

Boomer didn't want anything to eat, but he did have a bowl of soup before Uncle Petrie took him home. As he left, he asked Timmy, "What do we do now about the Indian relics and the Cherokee Treasure, Tim?"

"I'll finish up my map," Timmy replied. "Then we'll be ready for the expert when he comes along."

Boomer nodded, said good night, and headed for home.

Both Timmy and Lassie were tired out, but Ruth and Paul would not think of sending the boy to bed until Uncle Petrie returned. They wanted to talk about the day's trip on the mountain. Lassie settled down behind the stove and enjoyed her food.

Uncle Petrie came in rather slowly. The day had been a hard one for him. He looked at the group around the table and remarked, "That was my last trip up Kingpin Mountain."

Ruth smiled. "We were beginning to think it might be the last trip for all of you."

Lassie yipped as though this were an insult to her, and Timmy said soberly, "We really had nothing to worry about as long as Lassie was along."

"Any news about the bank robbery?" Uncle Petrie asked Paul.

"I'm afraid the law officers haven't come up with very much," Paul replied. "The captured man still won't say anything. And the check on his fingerprints and photograph hasn't brought any help from other police forces."

"Didn't the road blocks stop the car?" Uncle Petrie inquired.

"No luck there, either. The sheriff is sure that they didn't get out of the area by highway, but that means he ought to be able to find the car abandoned somewhere nearby. And they haven't found it. Bob Hanson had all of the cash checked—the loss is more than eighty thousand dollars."

Timmy was drowsing in his chair. Lassie came up from behind the stove and put her muzzle on the small boy's lap as if she had something to tell. But right now the talk about the bank robbery was of small interest to Timmy. He was afraid the older folks were forgetting all about the Lost Cherokee Treasure, the arrowheads and the spearheads.

Finally Uncle Petrie and Paul stopped talking and Timmy saw his chance.

"Do you think he'll really come?" he asked.

"Who?" Paul asked.

Timmy looked from his father to his mother, and she came to his rescue.

"The Indian expert, of course. Timmy doesn't care anything about your old bank robbers. He did his part of the job when he told Lassie to move in on them. Now he has work of his own to do."

Paul put a hand on Timmy's shoulder. "Honestly, Timmy, I can't be sure whether he's coming or not. If he thinks the things you've found are interesting enough, and different enough, he'll be here. If this adds something to what people want to know about the American Indians, he'll surely be out. I don't want to promise you anything and then not see it happen."

Timmy shook his head. He understood. This was grown-up business. He would have to let the grownups handle it in their own way.

"I think I'll go to bed." Timmy took the map of Kingpin Mountain from his pocket and headed for his room. Lassie followed close behind him.

"Don't worry," Uncle Petrie called after them. "That Indian expert is coming right out here to the Martin farm. I'm sure of it. I've got a hunch he's on his way from Washington right now. Just you wait and see. He'll want your map too."

"Thank you, Uncle Petrie." Timmy was tired but happy. "Good night," he said to all of them.

The next two days were lazy ones. Uncle Petrie and Timmy worked on the map of the Indian sites, and Boomer came over now and then to help them. It was obvious, though, that the older boy was losing interest.

"Couldn't we go fishing while we're waiting for this Indian expert to get here?" he asked.

Timmy was still excited about the relics and would hear of nothing that might take him away before the good news came. He was so sure it would come!

And then it did. At about four o'clock on the afternoon of the second day, the telephone rang in the Martin kitchen and Ruth answered it. It was Lottie Crane, the Capitol City librarian.

"Is Timmy there?" she asked.

"I'll get him," Ruth replied. She called Timmy in from outside and pushed a chair into place so he could reach the telephone.

"Good news, Timmy," Miss Crane said. "The Smithsonian Institution is sending out an expert. He should be here in a week or ten days. He must be an important man, because he's a college professor. Professor Harry Larkin, his name is."

"That's good!" Timmy replied quickly. "Did he say anything about us? Can we help him? Did you talk to him? Do you think we can go along with him?"

Lottie Crane knew how excited Timmy was. "I didn't talk to the professor, Timmy," she replied, "but I did talk to the people at the Smithsonian. They told me that the professor would not have any money to hire assistants. But these scientists do like to have local helpers."

"Would they want boys?" Timmy asked with a worried frown.

Miss Crane hesitated. "Well, you might ask your father about the Dead Sea Scrolls, Timmy. He'll tell you then what scientists think about boys, even small boys. I'm sure you and Professor Larkin will get along splendidly . . . . Do you mind if I give the story to the newspapers?"

Timmy turned to his mother and Ruth took the telephone.

"I think a story might be all right," she said. "But I wouldn't say much about the location of the Indian relics. I don't think Paul would want every local boy running all over our farm."

"I understand," Miss Crane replied. "I'll take care of it. We don't want to spoil things for the professor even before he gets here."

When Ruth hung up the telephone she saw Timmy roughing up Lassie's coat.

"He's coming," he was whispering. "Oh, the Indian expert is coming! We'll find that Lost Cherokee Treasure, Lassie—I know it!"

"Of course you will," Ruth assured him. "But I think we'll have a lot of things to do to get ready between now and the time Professor Larkin gets here."

Timmy grinned.

"I'm going over to Boomer's and tell him the news."

He hurried off on his bicycle. Boomer met him in the yard and was excited by the impending arrival of the expert. But Timmy noticed that Boomer was upset about something.

"Do you feel okay?" Timmy asked his friend quickly.

"I feel all right," Boomer replied. "But I'm afraid my father isn't going to let me go with you and the Indian expert to hunt for relics."

"Why not?" Timmy demanded.

Boomer tried to explain, but he didn't make a very good job of it. Then Mr. Bates came along and Timmy put the question directly to him.

"Can Boomer go treasure hunting with me when the Indian expert gets here?"

The farmer realized how important it was to Timmy. "I'd thought of coming over to your house tonight and talking to your father about that," he said. "Let's let it go till then."

And Mr. Bates did come over to talk to the Martins, late that night after Timmy had gone to bed. But the boy and his collie were wide awake. Timmy had grown so used to doing everything with Boomer that any pleasures without him would be spoiled.

"I think it will be a great experience for the two boys," Paul told Boomer's father.

"There's no doubt about that," Mr. Bates agreed. "The thing is, I've been planning on Boomer working on the farm this summer. He'll learn a lot about the work, and it will help him when he's old enough to have his own place."

Paul nodded. "But he's still a little young to worry about a farm of his own, don't you think? And a chance to know something about the Indians around here is nothing to throw away. I think it will do Boomer more good than farm work."

Mr. Bates considered for a few minutes. "Well, I suppose it would be good for Boomer at that," he agreed. "He's a fine boy, and he's been a big help around the farm all year. I guess I can get along without him for a while this summer."

The talk was interrupted by the sounds of a car driving up at the side of the Martin farmhouse. Timmy slipped out of bed and hurried over to the window. Lassie pattered along beside him and rested her forepaws on the sill.

"It's the sheriff!" Timmy cried. "Maybe he's found the bank robbers!"

He watched Sheriff Bert Casey leave the car and hurry up to the kitchen door. Then he climbed into his clothes quickly and pulled on his shoes.

Ruth answered the door while Paul and Mr. Bates looked up from the table. When Paul recognized their visitor, he jumped to his feet.

"What is it, Sheriff? Have you found anything?"

"Plenty," Bert Casey told them. "We've found the getaway car!"

"Where?" Paul inquired.

"In the the bottom of a water-filled quarry, about two miles from your farm, on an overgrown dirt road. These robbers must have gotten lost. They'll still be on the mountain. I'd like to borrow Lassie for a trailing job."

7 THE TRAIL OF THE BANDITS

Paul Martin was not surprised to find Timmy up and dressed. He bent down and patted Lassie. Then he said, "Timmy, the sheriff has a job for Lassie. He has found the car the bank bandits used, and he thinks Lassie may be able to pick up their trail across Kingpin Mountain."

The boy looked at his dog proudly. "She'll find them, all right. I know it."

They followed the sheriff out into the yard and he brought some clothing from the back seat of his car. They were the clothes that had been worn by the prisoner Lassie had helped capture. The sheriff hoped this would give the dog the scent of the others.

"There ought to be plenty of sign around the car," Mr. Bates pointed out.

"The water probably killed most of it," Sheriff Casey

replied. "But we'll check on it. We've lost enough time on this chase already."

Lassie went over to the clothing and took a good sniff at the garments. Then the collie crossed the yard, moved in among some low bushes, and headed across the small wood lot at the far side of the farmyard.

"Where's she going?" Sheriff Casey wondered. "I planned to take her to the quarry in the car."

Timmy watched Lassie for a moment. "I have a hunch Lassie will be at the quarry ahead of us," he said.

Paul, Ruth, Mr. Bates, and the sheriff all looked at the boy. Then they climbed into the car and the sheriff headed out of the Martin yard. Uncle Petrie, dead tired from the day's work, had already gone to his room.

Timmy was sitting between his mother and father. When they reached the main road and headed for the dirt lane leading into the quarry, Paul finally asked, "Exactly how do you know what Lassie is going to do, son?"

"I don't know for sure," Timmy replied promptly. "But I *think* Lassie has been trying to lead us somewhere for two days. We wouldn't follow her."

The sheriff turned into the side road and bumped along at a good speed. The cars which had come in ahead had broken down some of the bushes and opened a wider route. Just behind them they heard another vehicle coming.

When they finally stopped beside some police cars and a wrecker close to the lip of the quarry, Paul climbed out and looked back.

"By golly!" he said. "It's our pickup truck."

Timmy laughed. "And Uncle Petrie is in it. He's not going to be left out, even if he *is* tired."

They all chuckled as the older man braked the truck and came running up to them.

"What's going on here?" he demanded. "Trying to run out and leave me?"

"We thought rest would be better for you," Paul told him.

They walked ahead to the edge of the pit. The getaway car was on the end of a cable and being leveled off.

Lassie was standing close by. She was covered with dust from her trip through the woods; her coat was matted with brambles, and burrs were all over her long ruff.

Uncle Petrie looked at the dog for a moment, then snorted, "That dog's a heap smarter than all of us put together. She's just been waiting for us to catch on."

The sheriff came up. "What do you mean, Uncle Petrie?" he asked.

"Lassie was in that getaway car when it was run into the quarry," the old man explained. "She got out of it and came home to our farm, not long after the bank bandits headed into the woods with the stolen money. Lassie tried leading us back here that very night, but we wouldn't listen to her. Or *I* wouldn't. If we had paid attention to her then, we might have been a lot closer to the robbers than we are right now."

Sheriff Casey looked from Uncle Petrie and the Martins to the collie. Then he asked, "If Lassie was locked into the getaway car by the bandits, how did she get out?"

Timmy chuckled. "That's one of Lassie's favorite tricks—opening latches. She's able to open the door of the pickup and any other car door I've ever seen."

"She's a wizard at opening screen doors and window latches too," his mother broke in.

Sheriff Casey was convinced. Lassie, unaware of the excitement she had created, was sniffing around the still-dripping car. Casey walked over to her.

"I guess it doesn't make too much difference how she got out of the auto," he commented. "The important thing is that she did. And if I'm right about a smart dog like Lassie, she's not going to forget the men who tried to send her over that cliff in the car. She looks as though she's ready to pick up the trail right now. Let's get busy and follow her."

Timmy called to Lassie. Uncle Petrie went to the pickup truck and brought back a leash. It would make it easier to keep up with the dog on a nighttime trail.

Timmy looked up at his father. "May I go?"

Paul turned to Ruth. She opened her mouth to say something, then nodded.

"I'm sure he'll be all right," Paul said. "I was thinking about you."

"I'll be all right too," Ruth assured him. "I'll stay here with the men who are working on the car, and if they decide to take it back to town, I'll drive home in the pickup truck. Don't you worry about me."

The matter was left that way, and the sheriff and his men started off behind Uncle Petrie and the collie. Paul and Timmy were in the lead and talking excitedly about the chase. Most of the men were commenting on the miraculous escape of Lassie from the wrecked car.

The big collie set a determined pace, but there were times when she slowed down and cast from one side to the other. Sometimes the reason for her actions was apparent to all. Once Timmy was almost frightened stiff when he heard a loud, piercing scream. It sounded like a woman in agony.

Lassie sniffed the air, and the possemen with rifles clicked them into full cock. Timmy gripped Paul's hand tightly and whispered, "Who's that?"

"I guess it's a mountain lion," his father replied. "He's probably hunting with his mate. I guess he's killed a deer and wants to let her know about it, so she can come and share the meal."

Timmy shuddered.

Satisfied that the posse was not interested in the mountain lion, Lassie resumed her tracking, and about half an hour after leaving the quarry she led the way into a small clearing. The men turned their flashlights on the ashes of a campfire in the center of the space. Timmy had his own light and began prowling around.

Casey and his men looked for new clues. One of them picked up some crumpled papers and boxes; then Timmy found a shopping bag with scraps of food in it. Lassie came over and sniffed these.

"I reckon they stayed here overnight, all right," Sheriff Casey decided.

Timmy showed him the shopping bag. "Does this tell you anything?"

Bert Casey read the printing on the bag. It said, BAILEY'S SUPERMARKET, LEWISTON.

"If it says what it means," the sheriff replied, "then these fellows bought it on the other side of Kingpin Mountain. There's no direct road from here to there. Checking with Bailey won't do much good right now. He might recognize the fellow we have in jail, but he can't tell us where the others are tonight. Let's go, Lassie!"

Lassie jumped up and started out of the clearing on the far side. The dog and the men were grateful for the short rest but determined to carry through the chase.

Uncle Petrie, hurrying along behind the dog, was in his glory. Several times Paul thought of relieving the older man, but he realized one thing. Uncle Petrie was pacing the posse to his own strength; this meant that he was moving more slowly than one of the other men might travel.

The mountain trail was rough, but Timmy's enthusiasm carried him along for another mile or so. Then he began lagging behind. Paul looked at him.

"Do you want to head back, Timmy?"

The boy shook his head.

"Shall we wait here for Uncle Petrie and the others to come back?"

For answer Timmy lengthened his stride and half-ran to keep his place. Paul patted him on the shoulder and said, "I like your spunk, son. But I'm going to give you a piggy-back ride on the way down the hill. All right?"

Timmy laughed and agreed. "I always try to keep up

with Lassie—but when it comes to hiking, she has twice as many legs as I have."

"That she does," his father replied. The sheriff's men chuckled.

Timmy had been trying to recognize some of the landmarks in the darkness. The moon was up now and the stars were lighting the late night sky. Suddenly the boy called, "Uncle Petrie, isn't that Sentinel Rock?"

"It sure is," Uncle Petrie replied.

"Then we were right up here near them the other afternoon," Timmy said.

Sheriff Casey agreed. "I reckon we were pretty close to them too. But we just didn't know it."

They moved on from Sentinel Rock to the Indian caves. Lassie halted near these and began sniffing around among the rocks; finally she went into one of the caves. Uncle Petrie and one of the possemen followed her while Timmy and Paul stood at the entrance and looked inside.

"They've been in here all right," Uncle Petrie announced. He pointed to piles of brush and dried grass that had been made up as beds.

Sheriff Casey shook his head slowly. "I don't understand. Why would they camp only a short distance down the trail and eat a meal, if they were going to camp here overnight?"

Paul, Uncle Petrie, and the others considered this for several moments. Then Timmy said, "There might be one reason. I've been thinking about it ever since Uncle Petrie and Boomer and I climbed the mountain the other day. Strangers never come over this mountain. One of the bank robbers must be someone who lived around here, and maybe he camped here *before* the bank robbery. You know, to kind of look around for a hide-out so it would be ready when they needed it."

Sheriff Casey slapped his hands together. "I think Timmy's hit on something!" he exclaimed. "One of the men could have driven the getaway car into Capitol City, and the local man and his henchman could have come over the mountain to make sure the getaway trail was open for them. They could have camped here in this cave until it was time for the driver to meet them at the quarry and take them to the bank."

"Well, at least that gives us something to work on," Paul declared.

"Something," Sheriff Casey agreed, "but not enough. Let's go, Lassie!"

Since the caves were almost at the top of Kingpin Mountain, the route now was mostly downhill in the direction of Lewiston. This made the going a bit easier. Finally Lassie brought them out onto another dirt road which led into the main highway. He halted in a clump of willows where clear signs showed that an automobile had been parked for some time.

"I guess this is the end of the trail for the time being," Casey said briskly. "If this wasn't their getaway car, they could have escaped in several other ways. They could have hitchhiked out of the neighborhood, or walked down to the highway and taken a bus. But they'll be back."

"What makes you say that?" Paul asked in surprise.

"I've had that hunch for a long time," Sheriff Casey replied. "For one thing, that money, mostly in small bills so they could spend it, made up into two pretty big bundles. They wouldn't be able to make any time across Kingpin

Mountain carrying it all the way, with us covering the hills. And they'd look pretty suspicious toting it around with the name of the Capitol City Farmers Bank stenciled on the front of it."

Uncle Petrie and Paul were not convinced.

"If they did have another car over here, they could keep the bags under cover," Uncle Petrie pointed out.

"I'd give you that if it weren't for one thing," Sheriff Casey said. "The fellow we have in the Capitol City jail! The two men we're following wouldn't want to take a chance on this boy's turning State's evidence against them. He might identify them before they got across Kingpin Mountain, and if he did, and they were caught with the money, they'd be tied in with the robbery right away. And they'd lose the loot too! I'm sure they hid the money somewhere on the mountain. One way or another they'll be checking up on their jailbird friend. If they find out that he's keeping quiet, then they'll come back for the money and do their best to get him out of jail."

The men agreed there was some merit to this reasoning. Then Sheriff Casey looked over his tired companions and declared, "I think we've done enough hiking for tonight. It'll be daylight in an hour or so. I'll trot down to the highway and phone for one of the cars to come and pick us up."

As Casey started out, the other men and Timmy settled down beside Uncle Petrie and Lassie at the side of the road. Timmy was tired, but his head and his heart were still filled with thoughts of Kingpin Mountain and its connection with the Indians. He turned to his father and drowsily asked, "Daddy, what are the Dead Sea Scrolls?"

Paul studied the sleepy lad in surprise. "What makes you think about something like that at a time like this, Timmy?"

"I've been thinking about that Indian expert who's coming to town," the boy explained. "When I asked Miss Crane whether boys like Boomer and me could help find the Lost Cherokee Treasure, she told me to ask you about the Dead Sea Scrolls. So I'm asking."

His father smiled. "Lottie Crane was trying to tell you that little boys sure can help with something like this. The Dead Sea Scrolls are manuscripts that were written in the days of the Bible. They were found in a cave in Asia Minor by two small Arab boys who were herding goats."

"Did they have a dog?" Timmy asked sleepily.

"I'm sure they did. Maybe one a lot like Lassie."

Lassie lifted her head and barked sharply. It was pleasant to hear voices she loved, speaking her name in the darkness.

8 THE TREASURE SEARCH BEGINS

The disappointed posse returned to Capitol City and Calverton after daybreak. The Martins' car had been brought into town and Paul Martin drove it home with Uncle Petrie and a sleeping Timmy in the front seat beside him. Ruth had a warm meal ready for them, and they finished it before doing necessary chores. Then they all turned in to sleep.

The rest of the week moved slowly for Timmy and Boomer. The Bates boy was disappointed because he had missed the night journey across Kingpin Mountain, but Uncle Petrie assured him there would be a lot of excitement ahead when the Indian expert began the search for the Lost Cherokee Treasure.

It was about ten o'clock on Saturday morning when the big moment arrived. An automobile drove up in front of the Martin farmhouse. Timmy, who was cleaning his room, looked out of the window and saw the car pulling in. He began spelling out the words on the side of it. They were printed in the form of a shield and said:

U. S. GOVERNMENT
DEPARTMENT OF THE INTERIOR
BUREAU OF INDIAN AFFAIRS

FOR OFFICIAL USE ONLY

Timmy tumbled out of the open window, landed on his feet on the lawn, and ran toward the car. Lassie followed him with a little more dignity and hurried up to the newcomer. Ruth Martin, busy in the kitchen, heard the excitement and hurried to see what was happening.

The man who climbed out of the car was a tall, rather broad-shouldered fellow. He wore a pair of glasses with horned rims and tinted lenses. His hair was sparse and barely showed under a storm hat of plastic. He looked at Timmy and asked, "Is this the Martin farm?"

"Yes, sir," Timmy replied. "Are you Professor Larkin?"

U.S. GOVERNMENT
INTERIO
INDIA

"That I am, that I am," the newcomer agreed quickly.

Lassie had arrived by this time, and she was sniffing the visitor and walking around him as if trying to make up her mind about him. After she had completed her examination, she barked as though she weren't sure whether she should be friendly or not. Then Ruth Martin arrived. She greeted the professor pleasantly and invited him inside.

Timmy and Lassie followed along. Timmy wasn't sure that he liked the idea of his mother taking charge of the Indian expert, but he decided not to argue the matter. Instead he hurried to the phone to tell Boomer the big news about the arrival of the man from Washington.

Boomer and Mike arrived at the Martin farm within ten minutes. By that time Uncle Petrie and Paul had come in from their work for lunch, and they met the visitor. The conversation centered on general subjects while everyone got acquainted.

Finally Timmy could hold back no longer. "Professor, now that you're here, when are you going to start looking for the Lost Cherokee Treasure?" he asked eagerly.

"Treasure? Treasure?" Professor Larkin repeated the

word in some surprise. "Is that what I've come for?" He took his glasses off and polished them. Timmy and Boomer studied him, bewildered

Paul tried to explain. "I don't suppose Miss Crane told the professor about the possibility of the Lost Cherokee Treasure being hereabouts. He's merely interested in the things you've found at the pond."

Professor Larkin turned to Paul gratefully. "Exactly, exactly. That's all the information I have. But if there *is* a treasure, we certainly want to find it, don't we, Timmy?"

Timmy was relieved. "Then you do want Boomer and me to go along with you, and show you where to look for the things, Professor?"

"By all means," Professor Larkin agreed. "I would think that the menfolk would be busy at this time of the year, with crops and all. And you boys would be a big help to me. A big help, indeed."

Paul Martin looked at Ruth and they both nodded.

"I'll be glad to help down here around the farm and at the pond," Uncle Petrie said. "But I don't think I'm fit to go up that mountain again."

"I'll value your help, Uncle Petrie," Professor Larkin replied. "Miss Crane's letter said a lot of nice things about you. We ought to have a long talk before I start my search."

"Sure thing," Uncle Petrie replied. "There's half a dozen old-timers in my checkers-and-cribbage group. They're the only ones around here who know very much about the Indian days. You might like to talk to them too. They'll be getting together tonight."

Timmy was growing worried. "All this talking won't hold up the search, will it?" he asked.

Professor Larkin smiled. "Now that I'm here, I'm just as anxious to get started on this search as you are. Why don't we plan to begin looking tomorrow?"

"Tomorrow's Sunday," Boomer broke in.

Professor Larkin nodded. "I think we can look around that pond in the afternoon when you get home from church. Maybe we'll be ready to tackle Kingpin Mountain on Monday or Tuesday."

After lunch the professor put his car away in the barn, then spent most of the afternoon in the room which Ruth had set aside for him. Uncle Petrie, Timmy, and Paul were busy with the late afternoon chores.

As Lassie was coming in with the cows, Paul said, "This Indian fellow is certainly a big shot. I don't know much about things like this, but I'm sure I've seen his picture somewhere. I even have a hunch that I've met him too. But I guess I wouldn't remember about it—I was never very interested in Indians until these things turned up here on the farm."

"Lassie acts as though she's seen him somewhere before too," Timmy commented.

Paul chuckled. "I didn't know that Lassie looked at pictures in the papers."

The big collie barked briskly at the mention of her name.

Sunday afternoon the Martin farm was the scene of great activity. Professor Larkin had met the old-timers in the checkers-and-cribbage club on Saturday night, and now they were all on hand with Uncle Petrie to offer advice and suggestions as the professor and the two boys, dressed in old clothes, dug diligently around the edge of the pond.

Lassie carried on her own activities with a prodding nose

and two flying forepaws. As they cleared away the dried grass and the topsoil, other Indian relics were uncovered. Timmy exclaimed happily with each new discovery. Uncle Petrie examined the articles with interest.

There were any number of spears and arrowheads; then several tomahawk stones, in almost triangular shape, came to light. Soon the searched area ran right down to the edge of the water.

"Professor," Uncle Petrie said, "it begins to look like these things might go right down under the water. Why don't I drain the pond into the creek and let you get down a bit deeper?"

"A good idea, Uncle Petrie, a good idea!" Professor Larkin replied expansively.

Uncle Petrie let out most of the water, leaving just enough to take care of the fish and the ducks, with some drinking water for the stock as well. Timmy and Boomer worked briskly with their shovels, and suddenly Timmy turned up a big, heavy stone with a depression in the center. Close by he found another piece of stone which resembled a wooden potato masher. He pointed these out to the professor who was working close by.

Larkin glanced at them but did not show any particular interest. Timmy turned to Uncle Petrie and offered him the two objects. The old man patted him on the back, then announced to the oldsters, "This is really something!"

"It looks like one of them gadgets the druggist uses for rolling pills," commented one old-timer in a cracked voice.

"I don't think these Indians ever heard of either druggists or pills," Uncle Petrie replied. "I'd say they used this for grinding corn or other grains. I've seen pictures of things like this from Mexico and our own Southwest."

When about a dozen other interesting discoveries had been made, Ruth Martin called to the searchers from the farmhouse.

"I think it's about time you menfolks called it a day," she said. "I've got something cool and refreshing here on the porch—and some good hot water for baths."

Timmy frowned. The idea of another bath didn't appeal to him; he had taken one only the night before. But he did admit that he was pretty well messed up. He wished he could be like Lassie. When she was through working at her corner of the diggings, she simply walked into the shallow pond, ducked herself a couple of times, and shook herself dry.

That evening they talked a lot about the Indian relics, but when they asked Professor Larkin about some of his other trips, he was not inclined to discuss them.

"I suppose you see so much Indian stuff in your working time, that you like to forget about it when you're resting," Uncle Petrie smiled. "I wouldn't blame you."

The professor nodded and yawned. Then he glanced at the clock. It was only a little after eight.

"We'll want to be getting started early in the morning," he said sleepily. "I think I'd like to go to my room."

"By all means," Paul agreed. "Good night, and have a good rest." Timmy and the others wished him good night, and the professor went to bed.

Uncle Petrie shook his head when the door closed behind the expert. "He's sure a strange man," he muttered.

"I guess digging around in the past makes you that way," Paul replied.

Timmy hooked his fingers through Lassie's collar.

"We'll be getting up early in the morning too, old girl," he said. "I figure we'd better be going to bed too."

When Timmy was undressed and under the covers a few minutes later, he was a little surprised to find that Lassie did not take her usual place at the foot of the bed or under it. Instead she remained up on the pillow alongside the boy.

"Are you trying to tell me something important, Lassie?" he asked finally. Lassie barked several short barks, and Timmy put an arm around her.

"Is it important? Is it about Professor Larkin? Is it?"

Lassie barked again. This time Ruth and Paul looked in, afraid something might be wrong. Timmy smiled and waved to them, and they went on to bed.

Finally Timmy had an idea. "Do you think Professor Larkin is likely to keep the whole treasure for himself when he finds it?" he asked his dog.

Lassie barked loudly.

"Then you really think we're going to find the treasure," Timmy laughed. "Good for you! Now let's sleep on it."

The boy and his dog were asleep moments later.

They were both up bright and early the next morning,

helping Uncle Petrie and Paul with the chores. Professor Larkin came from his room in time for breakfast. He was dressed in rugged clothing, with hiking boots, and a strong walking stick was in his hand. He had a knapsack on his arm and did not look much like the meek and mild figure who had arrived on Saturday.

Uncle Petrie, Paul, and Timmy studied him with new respect. They all greeted him pleasantly.

"It's a fine, clear day," the professor declared. "I think it might be well to go up to Sentinel Point and the caves. That seems the most likely place to start our investigations."

"You mean Sentinel Rock," Timmy corrected him.

"That's it, that's it," the professor agreed.

"I can walk that far," Uncle Petrie decided suddenly.

"I'd like to have you along," Professor Larkin replied, "but I think it would be better if the boys and myself were the only ones who went into the Indian areas on this first trip. They are more likely to take my orders at all times," he concluded with a smile.

"I just don't want you to get lost," Uncle Petrie said.

Timmy felt sorry for Uncle Petrie, but he did not want

to lose his own chance of going along with the Indian expert.

"I've got the map, Uncle Petrie," he said quickly, "and we'll have Lassie along with us."

Professor Larkin turned to Timmy then and declared, "I think it would be better if the dog stayed home too."

"Lassie, stay home? Why, she wants to go as much as I do!" Timmy exclaimed.

"I can believe that," Professor Larkin replied warmly. "And she is a wonderful dog. But Uncle Petrie tells me that she dug up some of the first things you found out at the edge of the farm. She did quite a bit of rooting around yesterday too. If she starts digging where there are some really valuable relics, she might damage them. You understand that, don't you?"

Timmy looked at Ruth and Uncle Petrie. Finally his mother said, "We all agreed that the professor would be in charge of this Indian business. If he doesn't want Lassie around—and I can see that his reasons are good— I guess we'll have to tie her up in the barn and keep her there."

The matter was settled. They turned back to their breakfast, and Uncle Petrie livened it up with stories of the Indians on Kingpin Mountain—stories which he hoped would help Professor Larkin in his work.

Boomer Bates arrived in time for a large glass of milk and some fresh cookies which he ate while Ruth was preparing a big supply of food for the search party. Paul took Lassie to the barn so she would not be around when Professor Larkin and the boys took off on the trail up Kingpin Mountain.

Lassie sniffed and snorted as though she did not like the idea of being left behind. Paul looked down at her several times, then patted her on the head and said, "I'd feel much better if you were along too. But I guess if the professor has been climbing around in the Indian country out West, he's not going to let himself get lost on our Kingpin Mountain."

Lassie barked forlornly as though she didn't agree.

Timmy heard her barking as he and Boomer followed Professor Larkin from the farmyard toward the Kingpin Mountain trail. The boy's heart was heavy, but there was nothing he could do.

9 THE CAVE ON KINGPIN MOUNTAIN

Once they were in the woods and on their own, Timmy realized that he and his map were an important part of the search program. He took the paper out and unrolled it, then began marking the route they were to follow. Professor Larkin looked at it for a while, then made some signs on a map of his own that he was carrying.

"How long do you think it will take us to get there?" he asked.

"About an hour," Timmy replied.

They made good time along the trail, and only a little over an hour had passed when they came in sight of Sentinel Rock. Timmy pointed it out and the professor went over to look at it. He spent some time studying the river valley below.

"Very interesting," he said finally. "Certainly a wonderful place." He made some notes on his map, then turned back to the boys and commented, "Now for the cave!"

"Don't you think there might be some relics around Sentinel Rock?" Boomer asked. "With the Indians on guard there for so many years, they must have left some things around."

"I'm sure they did," Professor Larkin agreed readily enough. "But we can look for them on the way down. The caves sound as though they would be the big thing around here."

Timmy sided with the professor, and Boomer shrugged. They trudged on toward the caves. They had brought along lanterns and flashlights, and as they approached the entrance to the first of the caves, Timmy lighted one of the lanterns and handed it to Boomer. Then he struck a match and touched it to the wick of a lantern for himself.

Professor Larkin already had a large flashlight in his hand. He led the way into the cave, and they walked around inside for five or ten minutes. Larkin poked at piles of debris with the end of his walking stick and now and then uncovered things which the boys picked up.

Timmy and Boomer were watching the professor only occasionally. They felt sure that if he needed their help for anything, he would call to them. They were interested in their own search. If Professor Larkin wasn't excited about the Lost Cherokee Treasure, then Timmy and Boomer were determined to find it for themselves—if it was anywhere on Kingpin Mountain.

They lifted their lanterns, and suddenly Timmy cried, "Look at these pictures!"

The two boys held the flickering lanterns to the walls of the cave, and there they could see crude paintings in fading colors on the rocky face. One of them looked like a large buffalo bull running as a number of hunters with spears and arrows were closing in upon him. Another one showed an Indian with a leather snare, catching an animal like an otter as it slid down into the water.

The boys followed the series of pictures along the walls toward the rear of the main cave. At last Timmy said, "It must be getting cloudy outside. The mouth of the cave is getting dark."

Boomer laughed. "We don't have to worry about that

as long as we have our lanterns. They'll burn for hours yet."

The boys stopped looking at the pictures and began to assemble a number of the Indian relics that were on the floor and rocky shelves in the main cave. They came up with an interesting collection of battle-axes, war clubs, and rotting leather quivers. Some of the quivers were as stiff as boards, where they had been covered with sand and dried out. There were a number of pieces of pottery, too, similar to what they had already found at the edge of the muskrat pond.

When they had a good number of these gathered, Timmy called, "What shall we do with these things, Professor?"

"Make a list of them on the back of your map," replied the professor, "and I'll be back to help you in a little while."

The boys realized then that Professor Larkin had left the cave. As they looked toward the entrance, Timmy shivered.

"Hey, Boomer," he said, "it looks as though the opening is getting smaller."

"That's probably because the sun has gone behind a cloud," Boomer replied.

"Or it might be that someone is trying to trap us in here."

"How could anyone trap us?" Boomer demanded. "Your folks and my folks know we're here. Come on, Timmy! The professor gave us a job—let's get it done."

Back at the Martin farm, Lassie was struggling to get out of her prison. Almost as soon as Paul had left her tied in the stall and gone about his farm work, the collie had begun the job of freeing herself.

There were some friends of the Martins who might even have believed that Paul had deliberately made it possible for the collie to free herself so that she could go out to look for Timmy and his companions.

Lassie gnawed at the strap which Paul had used to fasten her, but she was soon convinced that she could not bite it through without taking quite a long time at the job, and tiring her jaws in the bargain. She stood up on her hind legs and discovered that she was able to reach the spot where the line was tied around part of the framework of the stall.

The collie worried it for a while, until the knot began to loosen. She released the tension on it, then moved up higher, got one of her teeth into the strands of the tie, and wrenched it open. When she settled back on the straw of the stall to rest, the line was coiled on the ground beside her.

She listened to discover whether any of the family were around. Ruth Martin would be in the kitchen, looking after the day's baking. Uncle Petrie and Paul were planning to work in the fields. Lassie moved around in the semi-darkness of the barn, found some fresh water in a bucket, and drank it. When her thirst was satisfied, she cleverly lowered the leather halter into the water and let it soak there.

After a while she began gnawing at the wet leather, and it shredded under her determined teeth. Then she heard a noise outside. A car was driving up and she knew that it was the sheriff's. The last time he had come to visit the Martin place, Lassie had been given a chance to chase around on the mountain for the night. But now she had

other business of her own to take care of.

With only a short piece of the leather strap now hanging from her collar, the big dog headed for the rear of the barn. She wriggled her way outside through a hay chute, crossed the open yard, and popped into the woods.

It did not take her long to pick up the trail of Professor Larkin and the two boys. She bounded along, and while her barking showed something of her sense of freedom, there was a certain amount of restraint in her actions too. She knew that she was disobeying Paul's orders, and she did not know how she would be punished if she were caught.

The trouble was, some inner feeling told her that Timmy and Boomer were in danger. She had to be where they were, so she could help them fight any enemy who might appear.

There were a lot of conflicting trails on Kingpin Mountain. Lassie had been this way three or four times, however, and she recognized the signs of her passing. The boys had been with her on two occasions, and now they were on the trail again. Lassie trotted along.

Finally she came to Sentinel Rock. She nosed around there and came up with strong sign of the man and the two boys. Then she turned in the direction of the caves. Her first instinct was to bark, but instead she crouched and looked ahead up the trail.

Lassie could see Professor Larkin working around the entrance to the main cave. But there was no sign of Timmy and Boomer. The scent of the boys led in that direction, but they were nowhere in view.

The collie straightened up. She knew from past experience that if the situation demanded it, she could handle a man like Professor Larkin. She did not know fear in a position like this one. She bounded ahead, and when she was about fifteen yards from the Indian caves she barked a greeting, as though glad to see the professor.

Larkin turned around and looked at the dog. He straightened up. Then he raised his stick as though he might be planning to strike her.

"Go home!" he cried. "You'll spoil things here! You'll be in the way!"

Lassie barked furiously. She recognized the menace of

the stick and backed off until she could decide just how she was going to fight against it.

She moved around the cave entrance in a wide arc. Professor Larkin did not leave his fixed position but turned to keep the collie before him. As she moved, Lassie caught the scent of Timmy and Boomer, and her senses told her that they were all right. But still she could not see them.

There is no telling what might have happened in the next few moments if there had not been another interruption. Lassie was the first one to realize it. Some men were coming up the trail from the direction of the Martin farm.

Moments later she knew that it was Sheriff Bert Casey and several other men. Lassie spotted them before Professor Larkin saw them and immediately scampered down the trail to meet them.

Casey petted the big collie.

"So this is where you are, young lady! The Martins guessed that you'd come looking for Timmy. Good dog, Lassie, good dog!"

One of the sheriff's companions was another old friend of Lassie's. He was Al Bronson, star reporter for the

Capitol City *News-Telegram*, the biggest newspaper in the county. His stories of some of Lassie's exploits had gone out over the press wires to other big newspapers in all parts of the country.

At the approach of the sheriff and the reporter, Professor Larkin's attitude changed immediately. He greeted the men pleasantly enough and introduced himself.

Bert Casey put out his hand. "I'm Sheriff Casey. This is Al Bronson—he's with one of our two county-seat newspapers, the *News-Telegram*. He's interested in doing a human-interest article on your work. If it proves to be as important as the Martins think it might be, he'll do a whole series on it. That ought to be a big thing for you, if it gets out on the press wires and to the TV and radio stations."

"Sure thing," Professor Larkin agreed. "But does the county sheriff always have time to take newspaper reporters all over the country chasing down stories?"

Bronson laughed. "This is a mixture of business and pleasure for the sheriff. He's chasing a couple of bank robbers. He lost them on Kingpin Mountain, so he spends a lot of time up here, hoping to pick up the trail again."

"Bank robbers?" Professor Larkin repeated in surprise. "Are they dangerous?"

"They scared the bank out of eighty thousand dollars," Bronson declared with a smile. "But I don't think they'd find much of a market for Indian relics."

"Some of them *are* pretty valuable," Professor Larkin commented.

Sheriff Casey smiled at this. Then he said, "Okay, Al. There's your expert. I imagine he's pretty busy, so you'd better get your story and then we'll be heading back to town. Where are the boys, Professor?"

Larkin looked around him as though he hadn't been paying much attention to Timmy and Boomer.

"I guess they're in the cave," he replied. "They found some things in there and were going to make a list of them for me."

Lassie had already made up her own mind that Professor Larkin would be occupied for some time with the sheriff and the reporter. She had gone looking for the boys.

Boomer and Timmy had their collection lined up before them across the floor of the cave like a regiment of tin soldiers. They were jotting down their own descriptions when Lassie's head and shoulders appeared in the narrow opening of the cave. The dog barked and the two boys turned to her.

"Lassie!" Timmy cried. "Lassie, what are you doing here?"

As he jumped up, Timmy kicked over one of the bowls, and it broke into several large pieces. The boy stared down in horror at what he had done. Then he turned accusingly to Lassie.

"Look what you've made me do! Professor Larkin told us you would cause trouble if we brought you along. Now look at that bowl. I'll bet it was one of the best things too."

Boomer examined the fragments.

"They're big pieces, Timmy," he said. "They'll cement together again. If Professor Larkin is a real *good* expert, he won't mind patching it up. I've seen lots of them in museums that are patched up. Some of Lottie Crane's things are patched up too."

"Just the same," Timmy said, "we'd better keep Lassie out of the cave. And we'd better go out with her, so she doesn't cause any more damage."

The two boys followed the dog out into the open air. They had to squeeze their way through the cave opening which had been partly walled up by Professor Larkin. Timmy looked at the narrow passage, then turned to Boomer and said, "I wonder why the professor is closing up the cave mouth."

"He probably wants to keep out animals like Lassie, or people who might interfere with our work," Boomer decided.

"The opening is so small now, he'll have trouble getting in and out himself," Timmy said.

"Maybe he has to make it small enough to put a large stone over it at night. I guess he'll tell us," Boomer concluded.

The boys were surprised to find Sheriff Casey and Al Bronson outside with the professor.

"How are you making out, fellows?" the sheriff asked.

"First rate," Timmy told him. "We've found a lot of relics, and there are picture stories on the walls. I'm going to trace some of them and take them home to Uncle Petrie.

He can't get up here to look at the pictures and study them like we can. And maybe Professor Larkin'll want them later on for his records."

Professor Larkin studied the boys. "Of course, of course," he replied. "They'll be very valuable."

He turned back to his interview with Al Bronson, while Timmy and Boomer continued talking to the sheriff.

"Between the professor and Uncle Petrie, I'll bet we can find out just what the picture writing means. It might lead us right to the Lost Cherokee Treasure. Don't you think so?" Timmy asked.

"Maybe," agreed the sheriff. "But I notice the professor has been blocking up the cave. Any special reason for that?"

"He doesn't want animals or people disturbing the relics," Timmy said.

Sheriff Casey frowned. "I hadn't thought of that. I hope Al's story doesn't lead everyone in Capitol City and Calverton to look for the Lost Cherokee Treasure. I'll have to speak to him about that on the way home."

"You'd better," Timmy said seriously. "Boomer and I can take care of things—with Lassie helping now and then.

But any more people up here would be in the professor's way."

Professor Larkin and the reporter joined them then, and the Indian expert heard the last comment.

"The boy is right," he declared. "We're on a very important job here. We can't have sight-seers running all about the place. I'm sure you can limit this thing, Sheriff. If you would, I'd appreciate it. And I think the people in Washington would feel that you were being a big help."

"I'll take care of it," Sheriff Casey agreed. "I'm sure people would be in your way up here."

Lassie looked up at the lawman and barked sharply, as though she weren't one bit happy about the whole thing.

10 PLANS FOR THE TREASURE

When Al Bronson finished taking his notes, he turned to Sheriff Casey and said, "I think we ought to have a bite to eat, then start back down the mountain. It'll be dark before we get to the Martin place."

The sheriff looked at the sun, which was half hidden now by the distant hills.

"Timmy, have you boys got good, warm camping gear?" he asked. "Will you be all right up here on the mountain? Even though it's summer, it gets mighty chilly after dark."

"We've got our sleeping bags," Timmy replied.

Professor Larkin was busy with the coffeepot over the campfire, but he did not seem to be experienced with it. The sheriff started to help him, checking the food supply as he did so; he wanted to be able to assure the Martins that all was well on the mountain.

When they had finished eating, the sheriff asked, "Professor, is there anything we can do to help you with your work here?"

Professor Larkin looked thoughtful. "Well, perhaps," he replied. "We've found some very interesting items up here, and I've been trying to decide just how we're going to get them down to Lew—er—to Calverton."

While the two men talked, the boys took Al Bronson into the cave and showed him the paintings and the relics which they had collected and lined up for listing. When they came back to the campfire, the newspaperman asked, "Who started holing up the entrance to the cave?"

"Oh, I did that," Larkin replied. "I thought it might be a good idea to protect the discoveries from prowlers. Animals and hikers, you know. I've had trouble with them in the past, now and then."

"I suppose that is a smart thing," Bronson agreed.

Sheriff Casey nodded. "The other night when Timmy and I were on the mountain, we heard mountain lions. They like to hole up in caves like these."

Timmy and Boomer shivered. Lassie snarled as though

she would like to meet up with one of the big cats.

The question of transport for the professor's discoveries came up again, and the sheriff referred it to Bronson and the local men.

"We know that the trail we followed up here is too steep and dangerous to try to bring up a wheeled vehicle," the professor said. "I doubt whether even horses could do the job without taking the chance of breaking a leg—particularly on the slope between here and Sentinel Rock."

Al Bronson nodded. Then, after checking a few places on the downhill side, he said, "Pack mules ought to be able to do the job. But it would take us a couple of days to round up enough of them to do much good."

Professor Larkin frowned. "Well, I guess three or four days wouldn't be too bad," he said. "I'm planning on several weeks around here, but I would like to feel that my valuables were in a safe place."

"Of course, of course," Sheriff Casey agreed.

One of the deputies was making a survey of the plateau behind the "kingpin" which gave the mountain its name, and he came back to say, "I reckon we could get a helicopter up here, if we had to. It would be a lot more expensive than mules, but it would be a sight quicker too. Think so, Sheriff?"

Professor Larkin considered the suggestion, then replied, "I think the mules will do fine, gentlemen!"

Timmy, Boomer, and Lassie were interested listeners. Finally Lassie barked, and Timmy smiled as he said, "I think Lassie is trying to remind us that the Indians did it with dogs."

"Dogs?" Sheriff Casey asked. "You mean sled dogs? But that would take snow, wouldn't it?"

"No," Timmy explained quickly. "Travois dogs. Uncle Petrie told us all about it. All you need is two bags like our schoolbags, a leather strap, and some string. We've been practicing on Lassie ever since Uncle Petrie showed us how it was done."

Al Bronson was interested, for he saw some more human interest for his articles. "I'd like to see just how that works," he told Timmy.

Timmy and Boomer were glad to demonstrate; Lassie wasn't so eager but finally she submitted. Timmy got two of the knapsacks they had toted up the trail on their backs, found a leather strap and some pieces of string among the gear, and went to work. He adjusted the strap high up around Lassie's shoulders and fastened it firmly to her collar. Then he set the knapsacks across her back, tying them to the leather strap at one end and around her middle at the other end.

"Walk, Lassie!" he called.

The intelligent collie began parading around the fire, with the small packs high up on her shoulders and not interfering with her gait at all.

"That's not bad," Al Bronson declared. He brought out his camera and took a picture of the dog and her burden. "It sure looks as though Lassie could tote her own supplies if she was planning to stay up here on the mountain for any length of time."

Professor Larkin snorted.

"That might be all right for Indians who were hauling trinkets and beads and things like that. But it wouldn't do at all for the things we've found already, and those things we're likely to find when we get farther back into the cave. We'll have a heavy load."

Sheriff Casey agreed with the professor. "I guess the mules are the real solution, Al. We'll have them here in three or four days."

The men from town had another round of coffee, shook hands with the professor, wished him luck, and then bade good-by to the boys. Lassie sent them off with a loud bark.

"Aren't you going to take the dog back with you?" Professor Larkin inquired.

Sheriff Casey hesitated, and Timmy said, "I think Lassie would rather stay with us."

The sheriff looked at the professor. "I'm sure the Martins will feel much better if they know that Lassie is up here on the mountain with the boys."

After a moment Professor Larkin shrugged his shoulders as if he really did not care. But it was clear to all of them that he would rather the dog would go back.

As soon as the trio was alone, the boys went back into the cave. Lassie stayed outside as though she intended to keep an eye on Professor Larkin and observe his actions.

When they had moved toward the back of the cave,

Timmy took Boomer by the arm and asked, "Do you like Professor Larkin?"

"*Like* him?" Boomer asked. "How should I like him?"

"Well, I've been wondering whether he really knows so much about Indians. He acts to me like he doesn't know what he's doing most of the time."

Boomer shook his head slowly, then said, "He acts to me like he knows what he's doing *all* the time, but maybe he doesn't want *us* to know what he's doing!"

"When did you first notice it?" Timmy asked.

"When we were working down at the pond. You know how your mother told us that the experts take good care of relics and see that they're cleaned and wrapped and everything. Miss Crane at the library told us the same thing. But Professor Larkin doesn't seem to worry about that at all."

"You're right," Timmy said. "Even though he could have gotten all the straw he wanted in the barn, he didn't try to protect anything. And we have nothing up here on the mountain to wrap up the things that we've uncovered in the cave."

"Do you think one of us ought to run after the sheriff and tell him?"

Timmy thought about the matter for a moment, then shook his head slowly. "I don't think so. Maybe Indian experts aren't supposed to wrap up the relics until they're ready to move them. We don't know much about it—and we could be wrong."

"But what about Lassie?" Boomer wondered. "The professor didn't like the idea of having her along. Your dad had to tie her up. And when she did get up here, Professor Larkin wanted to send her down with the sheriff."

"That's right," Timmy agreed, "and maybe she's suspicious of the professor too. At least she's outside there keeping an eye on him. That makes me feel a lot better."

"Good old Lassie!" Boomer declared. Then the boys returned to their searching.

Professor Larkin called them when it was time for supper, and the hungry hunters did full justice to it. They hoped that the Indian expert would tell them something about his plans for the next day, but he said very little about the work. Both boys felt sure that he was thinking of someone, or something, far from Kingpin Mountain.

Timmy and Boomer were tired, so they rolled up in their blankets and settled down for the night with Lassie stretched out between them. Neither the boys nor the dog dropped off to sleep immediately, however. They all were anxious to keep an eye on Professor Larkin and see what he would do next.

They didn't have long to wait. After a few minutes, the expert took one of the lanterns and strolled off down the hill in the direction of Sentinel Rock.

Boomer stirred and whispered, "Do you think he's going to go away and leave us here?"

"I don't think so," Timmy replied. "Anyway, we'd know our way home, so there wouldn't be much danger."

Lassie came up on her forelegs and peered into the darkness with her keen eyes.

Professor Larkin reached the rock and leaned against it. He brought the lantern up alongside him, shielding it from the cave mouth and directing the rays out over the river valley in the direction of Lewiston.

"He's sending a signal to someone," Timmy muttered.

"A signal? But who would he know over there?" Boomer wondered.

"Why else would he be waving a lantern?"

"Well"—Boomer thought it over, "maybe—maybe Professor Larkin has heard about the scouts at Sentinel Rock who kept in touch with Indians all up and down the valley. He might be testing the signal system to find out whether it would work. These college professors are pretty smart men. They don't like to say something is true, until they've checked it."

"That could be," Timmy agreed.

"Maybe Professor Larkin brought along some other men to help him with the work. He wouldn't want to have them all climb up here to the caves unless there was something for them to do—I guess." Boomer relaxed as though he had the whole thing settled to his own satisfaction. He began breathing heavily and soon fell asleep.

Timmy dropped a hand on Lassie's shoulder, and a few moments later they were both asleep too.

Professor Larkin continued with his lantern signals from Sentinel Rock.

11 PRISON IN THE CAVE

The next morning dawned bright and clear, and the warm sun on their faces awakened the two boys. They were chipper and lively from their night's rest, and anxious to get going. Professor Larkin was still asleep so they did not disturb him. Lassie raced around the clearing, chasing the small ground squirrels and chipmunks until they lost themselves in the tall grass and low bushes farther down the hill.

Timmy and Boomer stirred up the fire, feeding twigs and larger sticks of wood into the still-hot coals. Then they got out a frying pan and Timmy began frying the bacon. Uncle Petrie had shown them a spring of cool water in the shelter of some of the rocks, so Boomer headed in that direction with the canteens and one of the cooking pots.

When he came back a while later, the canteens were

filled and slung over his shoulders, and the water was splashing over the top of the cooking pot. Timmy took the brimming pot and Boomer carried the canteens into the main cave where they would be out of the sun.

Timmy and Boomer hoped to join the cub scouts this year and they demonstrated their camping skills whenever they had the chance. Uncle Petrie had been encouraging them in this for quite a while. As the aroma of bacon and eggs came to the nostrils of Professor Larkin, it aroused him, and he sat up in his blankets. Finally he joined the boys at the fire and they ate a hearty breakfast.

Afterward Boomer cleaned up as Timmy turned to the professor and said, "I guess we'd better get busy in that Indian cave—don't you think so, Professor?"

Larkin shrugged. "There's no hurry. We can guess pretty much what's in there. I think I'll do a little exploring around the countryside. Maybe I'll spot something else of interest."

"Do you want us to come along with you?" Timmy asked.

"Not this time," Professor Larkin replied. "You've got

your work to do in the cave. I'll be back around noon. You do a good cooking job—maybe you'll have a nice lunch ready for me when I get back."

Timmy was flattered. He and Boomer lighted their lanterns and headed into the cave. Lassie watched them go, followed them as far as the partly blocked entrance to the cave, then turned back to keep an eye on Professor Larkin. When the professor strode off a few minutes later, swinging his heavy walking stick, Lassie gave him a short start, then pattered along behind him.

After another hour's work the boys had found all of the Indian relics that were close to the surface of the sandy cave floor. They went to get shovels, but as they were carrying them in, Timmy said, "This is the time the professor ought to be here. We might smash something valuable with the end of a shovel."

"You said it!" Boomer exclaimed. "Let's make a list of these things like the professor told us to do yesterday—then we'll wait for him."

When the listing was done, Timmy went to the fire and began making lunch, while Boomer continued with the job of tracing the picture writing on the walls. To reach one of the higher sections of a painting he had to climb up on a ledge. There, far back against the wall, he discovered some more pottery.

"Timmy, Timmy, look at this!"

Timmy set down the frying pan and came running into the cave. He was delighted with the new discovery.

"We can add these to our list this afternoon," he said as he examined the bowls and plates.

Professor Larkin came along then, with a dutiful Lassie following along behind him. The professor was sober-faced as he approached, but he smiled when he saw the boys working at the fire. They ate together, glancing occasionally at the clouding sky.

"I guess we're going to have a thunderstorm," Timmy said. "Sometimes they're pretty wild around here."

"I think the cave will keep us dry," Boomer declared.

They finished their lunch and the boys cleaned up. Professor Larkin and Lassie went on another journey outside the cave, but the threatening skies soon brought them back. When the clouds finally opened and dumped rain on them, they all hurried for the shelter of the main cave.

Safely under cover, Timmy and Boomer brought out their new finds. The professor examined them with mild interest, then pursed his lips and turned to Timmy.

"What do you know about this Lost Cherokee Treasure?"

Timmy was a little surprised that a great Indian authority like Professor Larkin did not know about the Lost Cherokee Treasure, but he told him as much as he could remember of what he had learned from Uncle Petrie and his dad.

"About how much would you say it was worth?" the professor asked.

"I don't know. Maybe a million dollars!" A million dollars had always been Timmy's idea of all the money in the world.

"A million dollars!" Professor Larkin whistled, obviously taking the estimate quite literally. "No wonder that Bronson fellow was interested in writing a story about it. It would be quite a feather in our caps if we came up with a discovery like that. One third of a million dollars!"

Timmy looked at Boomer, and some of their suspicions

of Professor Larkin evaporated. It certainly sounded as though the professor was inclined to give the two boys a full share of any discoveries they might make here on Kingpin Mountain.

The rain was over by then and Professor Larkin headed back out of the cave. Lassie looked at the two boys, then followed the man onto the rocky platform in front of the cave. With renewed enthusiasm, Timmy and Boomer scrambled up onto the shelf and began looking for more Indian relics.

While the boys were busy, Professor Larkin had plans of his own and he proceeded to carry them out. He walked around for a while to study the rain-washed area between the Indian cave and Sentinel Rock. Then he began collecting large boulders and carrying or rolling them to one side of the cave opening. When he had assembled enough of them, he began to set them across the entrance.

Unaware of their danger, Timmy and Boomer continued working. Lassie watched every move the professor made, but she did not try to do anything until Larkin put the final stones in place, blocking off the opening completely.

Then the valiant dog scrambled up onto the rocks and began trying to push them aside with her strong forepaws. Professor Larkin stood back and watched her for some moments.

"You're a mighty smart dog, Lassie," he commented cruelly, "but I don't think you're that smart."

The collie kept one eye on the man, but she still tried frantically to dislodge the stones and open the entrance to the cave. Professor Larkin strolled over to where his gear was piled neatly in the shelter of a smaller cave and began sorting out some things there.

Lassie's feelings were building up. Her instincts told her that Timmy and Boomer were in danger and that she had to do something about it.

She might leave this place and head back to the Martin farm to bring help as she had done on so many occasions before. Or she might attack Professor Larkin. But there was no one near to help her, even if she threw Professor Larkin to the ground and held him there.

There had been times in the past when Lassie had learned that it was sometimes best to play a waiting game.

On her own, she had often hunted animals in the woods and had spent hours at a time waiting for them to come along a game trail, return to a burrow, or head for a drinking place. This looked like one of those times when waiting would be the best thing to do.

Lassie decided to do her waiting as close to Professor Larkin as she could, so that he could not attempt to escape while Timmy and Boomer were trapped inside the cave. She moved over toward the Indian expert and hunkered on the ground close to him.

"So, Lassie," Larkin said briskly, "you're not going to fight those rocks any more . . . . The boys are in no real danger, you know. They probably don't even know that they are walled in. Until the lanterns use up all the kerosene, they won't realize that there is no light coming in from the outside."

He came toward Lassie, talking to her soothingly. But when he extended a hand, the collie backed away.

"They're in no real danger, Lassie," he repeated. "They've taken water in there with them. They took their packs inside before the rain started—and they can live there for several days or even a week if they have to."

Lassie barked sharply. Perhaps she thought it might attract the attention of Timmy and Boomer. Or maybe it was meant as a challenge to Larkin. The Indian expert merely laughed. He stopped about five feet from Lassie, then bent to go through his equipment again. This time when he stood up, he held something in both hands.

It was bundled up and Lassie had no way of telling what it was. But the professor did not keep her in doubt for very long. He was holding a snare which was not unlike a small fish net, and when Lassie came close enough to him, he extended it between his two arms and rushed toward her.

The collie did not realize her danger until it was too late. She tried to jump back, but Professor Larkin sprang forward, almost fell over the large dog, and entangled her in the mesh of the snare. The more Lassie moved and wriggled to free herself, the more firmly she became entangled in the net.

Finally she was almost exhausted, and her native intelligence told her that she would be much better off if she relaxed for a while and recovered her strength. When she had quieted down, Professor Larkin checked the net for rips, then strolled back to the entrance of the main cave.

He collected other and larger stones and heaped them on top of the pile he had already built.

A good part of the afternoon had slipped by. This time when darkness showed in the east, it was the early twilight of a cloudy day.

Inside the cave, Timmy and Boomer worked along, feeling pride and delight in each new discovery they made. It was almost six o'clock when the light in Boomer's lantern began to sputter out as the tank emptied and the wick became dry.

Timmy moved his wrist watch up against his own light.

"Golly, it's nearly six o'clock!" he exclaimed. "It's time to get supper."

Timmy was on the cave floor and his friend was up on the shelf, passing down the discoveries. When Boomer lowered himself from the ledge, he looked at Timmy and asked, "Which way is out?"

At first Timmy did not understand what Boomer was

talking about. Then he realized that with Boomer's lantern empty and his own burning up the last of the kerosene in its reservoir, things were becoming gloomy inside the main cave. Both boys looked for some sign of the irregular gray oval that would mark the opening through which they had entered the cavern.

Timmy shook his head. "I guess I don't know."

Boomer took Timmy by the arm. "What do you think is happening outside?" he demanded. "Why did Professor Larkin block up the cave entrance?"

"Maybe Lassie can tell us," Timmy choked. He raised his voice and cried, "Lassie! Lassie!"

They waited for several moments, holding onto each other in the first grim clutch of fright. Then they heard excited barking, but there was something unusual about it.

"At least Lassie hasn't gone away and left us," Boomer said in some relief. "I guess she doesn't know how to get in to us, though."

"At least we know the direction of the opening now," Timmy pointed out. "The barking came from over there. Lassie will be right outside."

He led the way to the front of the cave, and they walked along slowly in the shadowy cavern, side-stepping the Indian relics on the floor. Finally they came to the rough, inner side of the rock pile that blocked the entrance.

"Lassie! Lassie!" Timmy called. Lassie replied as well as she could, but again Timmy sensed that there was something wrong. He turned a pleading glance to Boomer and the older boy shrugged.

"Maybe the professor has her tied up, and she can't come to help us."

"Or maybe he's hurt her," Timmy worried.

"Hurt her? Why should he hurt her?" Boomer couldn't believe that anyone would want to harm the collie.

"Maybe he's afraid that she'll cause him trouble."

Boomer was more puzzled than ever. "What kind of trouble?"

Timmy was thinking about many things that had happened in the past week or so. He recalled Paul's conversation with Uncle Petrie when Professor Larkin arrived. His father had said something about recognizing the professor "from his pictures." Maybe Paul had seen the man in person. Maybe he had seen him in Capitol City at the time of the bank robbery!

"I think the professor came up here to get something that's hidden here," Timmy said finally.

"The professor?" Boomer asked. "What would he be hiding here?"

"I don't think he's a real professor at all!" Timmy said quickly. "I think he's one of the bank robbers, and they sent him up here to get the money they hid after the robbery!"

Boomer's mouth dropped open in amazement. He looked at Timmy closely to see if he was serious.

"The professor a bank robber?" he repeated.

"I'm not *sure,"* Timmy hedged, "but that's what I think. And I think Professor Larkin has tricked himself."

"How do you figure that?"

"Well," Timmy pointed out, "it's time for dinner, and all of the food is here in the cave with us. Professor Larkin hasn't anything to eat."

Boomer laughed. But it was a hollow laugh, as though the boy were not quite sure whether this was funny or not.

Timmy's stomach was more important to him than anything else right now. He headed for the food supply and the canteens, and soon he was assembling rations for Boomer and himself.

Boomer admired the way in which Timmy was meeting the situation, but as he ate, an unpleasant thought came to him.

"What are we going to do after we finish eating?" he asked. "I don't think I could go to sleep."

Timmy agreed. "I couldn't either," he admitted. "First of all we'd better call to Lassie to go for help. Then we'll be very quiet just as though we were going to sleep, but instead, we'll head for the front of the cave again and start to move those stones from the inside."

Boomer brightened. He put an arm around Timmy's shoulders. "Your mother and father are always telling me to look after you when Lassie isn't around," he said. "But it sure looks as though you're keeping an eye on me right now."

The two boys moved up to the rock barrier which kept

them prisoner. There were flickers of light coming in around the stones, and this reassured them that they would have plenty of fresh air.

Timmy cupped his hands over his mouth and called, "Lassie! Lassie!"

The big collie stirred in the net alongside the cave mouth about ten or fifteen feet from the boys. She barked excitedly. Professor Larkin looked across the fire at her and grinned.

"Go get Dad, Lassie!" Timmy shouted. "Bring Dad! Lassie, good dog, good dog!"

12 TROUBLE FOR LASSIE

Timmy and Boomer had no way of knowing that Lassie herself was held a prisoner and was in a much more serious situation than they were. Their belief that the dog was going for help gave them some peace of mind and made it possible for them to keep busy.

As soon as they had called to Lassie and she had responded, the two boys began working gingerly at the rock wall. They picked up one stone at a time, laid it aside carefully, then turned back for another one. They worked along without talking for nearly an hour. Gradually lines of light that marked the separations between the stones became wider.

Finally Timmy caught hold of one large rock and began tugging at it. When he could not move it by himself, he turned to Boomer.

"Give me a hand with this, will you? I think if we can move it out of the way, the opening will be big enough for us to crawl through."

The two boys were covered with dust, and their faces were streaked with a mixture of dirt and sweat. Their clothes were torn and stained. But their mood was cheerful. Boomer moved up beside Timmy and got his hands under the stone on the opposite side.

"One—two—three—pull!" Timmy counted.

Both boys yanked with a will. Seconds later they knew they were in trouble. The big stone began to move out of its position, but there was an awesome clatter as the stones above and beyond it also began to come away.

"Jump!" shouted Timmy, and the two boys leaped back into the darkness of the cave. Behind them there was a loud crash as the keystone they had been moving clattered to the floor, and literally hundreds of other pieces of rock and rubble came down behind it.

Now the cave mouth was blocked for good. Two small boys with hands and trench shovels would never succeed in breaking through it.

As the dust settled around them, Timmy turned to Boomer.

"I sure hope Lassie gets back with Dad before long," he said tearfully. "Otherwise, we're sunk!"

Outside the cave, Lassie had no way of knowing how much the boys were depending upon her. She had heard the orders to go for Paul Martin, but the bonds of the net held her. For about twenty minutes after the snare had dropped around her, she had tried to bite her way out of it. But when she had gnawed through several strands and had succeeded only in getting the net farther back onto her head without releasing her feet or the rest of her body, the collie realized that she was trapped.

Professor Larkin kept an eye on the dog for a while, then went around to his own supplies where, unknown to Timmy, he had hidden some food. Later he moved to one side of the cave mouth and began working away at a pile of stones. He had taken a good many of these for the walling job; now he cleared away the others to the soft ground beneath.

The man dug with one of the trench shovels until he had uncovered two canvas bags. Then he straightened up with a grin. The bags were dirty white, and on the outside of each one of them was the inscription:

CAPITOL CITY FARMERS BANK

Sight of the bags stirred something inside the mind of the collie. Her instincts had told her, on the Saturday before when Professor Harry Larkin had come to the Martin farm, that she had seen him and known him before. If she had had any way of communicating with Timmy and his father, she could have told him that the "professor" was the bank robber she had chased across the main street of Capitol City and into the getaway car. She had good reason to know him, for he had been the one who had slammed the car door at the edge of the stone quarry, hoping to drown the collie in a watery grave.

The bogus Indian agent, who looked as though he was about to complete the escape with the eighty thousand dollars belonging to the Capitol City Farmers Bank, was Bill Gates.

Gates worked carefully. When he had lifted the bags and shaken the excess dirt from them, he brushed them off thoroughly, then refilled the hole and covered it up with the stones so it would give no indication to the sheriff or his posse that anything had been buried there.

The bank bandit turned back to the collie then and knelt beside her. Lassie tried to bark, but Gates caught her by the jaws and held them tightly. He dragged the dog away from the cave, and when they were out of earshot of the boys, fastened a tight muzzle on her head.

He began working with the snare then, and as he cleared it from her front legs, he attached a sturdy leash to the dog's collar. Then he brought out some leather straps which he had hidden in his duffel in anticipation of his work on Kingpin Mountain.

Gates took one of the small knapsacks discarded by the boys after the experiment to demonstrate the use of a pack dog the day before, and he fastened this to Lassie's back. Then he dumped the contents of one of the moneybags into the knapsack.

"I think you'll be a big help to me, Lassie," he told the

dog. "You and I are going to work together."

The bank robber fastened the collie to a rock pinnacle and then began to assemble as much of his own gear as he planned to carry. The rest of it he hid in one of the smaller caves so it would not be obvious to anyone who might come searching for him and the boys.

He dropped the balance of the money and the empty bag into his own haversack, then swung it onto his shoulders, and picked up the collie's leash.

"Come on, Lassie, we're on our way!"

Whether Gates deliberately raised his voice when he called to the dog or not, the words carried to the ears of the frightened boys in the cave.

Both Timmy and Boomer were on the verge of tears. Only the faint hope that Lassie was bringing aid to them had kept them from breaking down completely. Now that it was clear to them that the dog was a prisoner, and unable to help them, they lost all hope.

"Lassie! Lassie! Lassie!" screamed Boomer.

"Professor Larkin!" called Timmy. "Let us out of here!"

A harsh laugh was the only reply they got from Bill

Gates—alias Professor Larkin. Then there were no more sounds from beyond the rock barrier.

Gates was congratulating himself on the completeness of his plans and the way in which they were working out. As he headed along the trail with Lassie he recalled, step by step, the development of the plot.

The robbers had learned about the impending arrival of Professor Larkin from the newspaper story which Lottie Crane, the librarian, had given to the Calverton *News,* the Capitol City *Spectator,* and the Capitol City *News-Telegram*. They had been reading the local papers to keep track of any developments in the case of Jack Crane, the jailed bank robber, and his missing partners.

Bill Gates knew that if he were going to make use of Timmy Martin and Boomer Bates to disguise his errand on Kingpin Mountain, he would have to consider Lassie. Both Gates and Jack Crane had good reason to know that the collie could be a dangerous opponent.

Even when the Martins had agreed to keep Lassie on the farm while the bogus Indian expert and the boys were on the mountain, Gates had realized that the collie was not the type of a dog that could be tied up for very long. He was glad now that he had brought along the snare, the muzzle, and the leash; they had come in handy. Without them he would have had to improvise bonds for Lassie from ropes and twine, and this would have delayed his escape with the hidden money.

Bill Gates was smugly amused by the twist of circumstances which had given him a chance to put Lassie to work. The idea was as pleasing to him as was the thought of the sheriff taking time out from the chase after the bank robbers to collect pack mules. He tugged at the leash and twisted Lassie's head to one side. The gallant collie growled, then grew silent as she realized her protest was giving cruel pleasure to the bandit.

Back on the hilltop in their cave prison, Timmy and Boomer settled down near their duffel. They were completely stunned by the capture of Lassie, and the departure of the man they knew as Professor Larkin.

After ten or fifteen minutes of complete silence all about

them, they began to hear rustlings in the darkness above their heads.

"What's that?" Boomer asked in a husky whisper.

Timmy shook his head. Then his face brightened and he replied, "Bats, probably. They're usually found in caves like this. Oh, boy, don't I wish Uncle Petrie was here!"

"Bats?" Boomer repeated. "Hey, they're dangerous, aren't they? They get into your hair and get it all snarled up. We're in enough trouble already!"

"Uncle Petrie always said that hair-snarling story was a big fairy tale," Timmy declared. "But there's one thing that bats really do—they go out hunting at night. I wonder what these bats are going to do about that, now that the cave opening is blocked up."

Boomer was like most boys his age. With something to do that was strange and interesting, he forgot all about any real difficulty he might be in. He picked up one of the flashlights and shone it on the roof of the cave.

Sure enough, there were a great number of bats hanging from the limestone ceiling, clinging there with the hooks on their feet and on their folded wings. As the light struck them, their eyes gleamed like brightly colored jewels. The tiny beasts tried to shield themselves from the rays.

Timmy picked up another flashlight. "At least we don't have to worry about light in here," he said. "Uncle Petrie took care of that. We've got enough flashlight batteries and bulbs to last us for several days. And there's some matches in a waterproof container."

"I sure wish Uncle Petrie was with us now," Boomer commented grimly. "But I guess we'll have to depend on the lights and the bats."

Timmy looked puzzled.

"What are you talking about?"

"Maybe if we watch the bats," Boomer explained, "they'll show us another way out of the cave."

"That's it!" Timmy thought quickly. "We can tell from the relics and the picture writing that the Indians who stayed here were pretty smart. I don't think they'd stay here in a cave with only one way out. They'd be trapped in a surprise attack by an enemy tribe."

Boomer nodded. "If they were using Sentinel Rock as a scout lookout, they'd have two or three ways out, I bet.

But how are we going to find them?"

Timmy thought for a while.

"I'm going to light up the passage as brightly as I can. Then I'll start searching for a blocked opening like the one at the main entrance. Maybe it won't be as thick, and we can dig through it. Let's go!"

"You start," Boomer replied. "I'm going to keep an eye on these bats. When they head out of here, I'm going to follow *them!*"

Timmy hesitated for a moment. "Okay," he said. "But there's one thing that might be bad for you."

"What's that?"

"The bats might know a way that's big enough for them, but too small for you and me," Timmy explained.

The two boys started looking in their own ways. Boomer kept an eye on the bats, but he also worked along the ledge on the opposite side of the cave from Timmy, searching for another way to the outside.

An hour later they were dead tired, and they had found nothing. Suddenly Boomer cried, "Look, Timmy, there they go!"

He pointed up to the ceiling in the direction of the bats. Sure enough, as the boy moved the beam of his flashlight along the limestone rock, it could be seen that the little, furry, flying beasts were forming into a moving stream and traveling toward the rear of the cave.

Timmy's mouth dropped open in amazement, and he stood beside Boomer and studied the migration. The bats took a route that carried them along the ledge on which the boys had been working during the afternoon. They flew out of sight through a black opening at the back of the cavern.

Timmy and Boomer hurried along until they were in that corner of the underground room, then scrambled up onto the ledge again. As they moved, their flashlights caught portions of the Indian paintings on the wall, and it occurred to Timmy that some of these drawings might tell a story about the Lost Cherokee Treasure itself.

He would investigate that later on. Right now he wanted to get outside and see the moon and the stars over his head. He wanted to shout for Lassie and hear her bark. More important, he wanted to run home to his mother and dad.

Timmy was a frightened boy.

Boomer was the first one up on the ledge. He crawled along through the darkness, came to the opening, and tried to thrust his shoulders through. When it was clear he was not going to succeed, he turned back to Timmy.

"You were right, Timmy."

"Right?" Timmy asked. "About what?"

"The bats can get through here, but we can't!"

Boomer backed up and they both hunched down on their knees before the opening. Timmy shone his light on the passage and studied it carefully. He looked at the surface of the shelf for some sign of debris that had fallen down, but there was little or none.

Next he moved back along the ledge a few yards and found the small trench shovel. He came back with this and began jabbing the sharp point of it against one corner of the opening. Pieces of limestone chipped away and fell down. The boys kept their mouths closed so that the dust which formed would not go into their lungs.

The passage was widened gradually, but it took a long time. Finally Boomer had an unpleasant thought.

"Suppose we're digging in here when the bats come back into the cave," he muttered.

"What about it?" asked Timmy. He was so tired he could hardly see what he was doing.

"They'll fly right into our faces," Boomer pointed out. "Ugh!"

Timmy laid down the shovel.

"Maybe we ought to quit until morning," he said slowly. "If we get a good night's sleep we'll feel better—and by that time the bats will be back."

Boomer licked his lips. He was lonesome and afraid, just as Timmy was, and he wanted to get out of the cave as quickly as possible. But he hated the thought of the bats returning while they worked.

"I think that would be a good idea," he agreed.

They started to back out of the passage connecting the main cave with the bats' exit. When they were clear of it, Timmy said thoughtfully, "That means that after we get through the hole, we'll have to wait until tomorrow night to follow the bats the rest of the way."

Boomer considered this.

"Why don't we sleep awhile, then check and see if the bats are back," he suggested. "If they're still out, we can try and break through in time to see how they come back in. Then we can get out through the opening." He yawned mightily.

Timmy decided this was a good idea. He recalled something Uncle Petrie had told them about the bats at the Carlsbad Caverns in New Mexico. Uncle Petrie had described how they left just after dark and came back just before daylight. They should be out hunting for many more hours.

The two tired boys found a good wide spot on the ledge, settled down, and soon dropped off to sleep.

Lassie was fighting a battle with herself as she moved along the trail beside Bill Gates. She kept dragging on the check leash and trying to turn back toward the cave. Inside her there was a constant struggle between her responsibility to Timmy and the knowledge that Gates was one of the men who had tried to harm her. She wanted to repay him for that.

When she had fought against the leash once or twice, Bill Gates lost his temper. He yanked on the leather, threw the collie off balance, and cried, "Heel, dog, heel! I didn't want you trailing along with me in the first place. But now that you're here, I'm going to see that you carry your part of the load. I'm not a softy like Sam Rowan. If you don't do as I tell you, I'll make you suffer for it!"

Lassie shuddered, more at the vehemence in Gates's voice than because she understood the meaning of his words. He showed clearly that he was mean and vicious, and might well harm the collie.

She looked back over her shoulder in the direction of the trail now clothed in darkness. At the other end, she knew, were a desperate Timmy and Boomer. But there was little or nothing she could do about it right now.

13 LOST IN THE DARKNESS

During the trip along the trail, Lassie had discovered one interesting thing. When she traveled alongside Bill Gates, or lagged behind him, he had control of the leash and of the harness which supported half of the stolen money. But when she ran ahead of him, she was able to lighten the burden of the collar and straps, and in this way she thought she might be able to loosen the burden upon her.

If she did this, Bill Gates would have to stop to adjust it, and the collie might have a chance to make a move toward escape. She found that there was a shift in the money knapsack when she struck the bags against trees or bushes along the trail, and therefore she swayed out in this way as many times as she could.

Because of the darkness, and the fact that the bank robber kept his light on the trail some distance ahead of them, he did not realize just what was happening.

They had traveled about three miles from the Indian cave and taken nearly an hour to do it, when suddenly Lassie began to stumble. Bill Gates brought the light back to shine upon the dog. He saw the harness and the money had shifted. He thrust his walking stick into the soft ground alongside the trail, then tied the leash around it and knelt beside Lassie to adjust the pack.

While he was working on this, and one of the straps was loose, the big dog saw her chance. With a snarl she leaped on his chest, almost bowling him over in his surprise, then jumped away into the darkness.

Bill Gates whipped out a pistol and began shooting haphazardly. Then he realized that the sheriff might still have posses on the mountain who would hear the gunfire. He crawled around on the ground to locate the flashlight he had laid beside him, finally snatched it up, and started after the fleeing collie.

"Come back here!" he shouted. "Lassie, come back!"

Lassie cut through the thick brush determinedly and put about a quarter of a mile between herself and the bank robber before she slowed down. But before she had covered half this distance, she realized that she was under a severe handicap. She had knocked off the muzzle, but the leash was dragging along behind her. Each time she tried to jump over a tree root or a low-hanging branch, she became entangled in the strap, and had to back up to free herself.

As she struggled, the collie could hear Gates blundering along through the darkness. After she had been pulled up short several times, she finally decided that the only solution was to get rid of the harness and the burden on her back. She settled down a few feet off the path and began snapping at the cords and leather straps around her shoulders.

Bill Gates was frantic at this sudden turn in his fortunes. Lassie could hear his cries in the darkness, though she did not understand what he was saying.

"When I catch that dog, I'll kill her!" he screamed.

He had to find her! The fact that she had carried off about forty thousand dollars of the stolen money was something that he could never explain to Sam Rowan and the imprisoned Jack Crane!

Lassie hunkered down in the shadows of the woods and battled her bonds.

A restless Timmy was fighting for his own freedom back in the Indian cave at the same time. He had been able to sleep only a short time; the excitement of his position was too much to allow him more.

Maybe some sixth sense told him that his beloved Lassie was in trouble too.

In any case, he climbed to his feet, looked down at the calmly sleeping Boomer, and decided not to awaken him. He moved along the ledge quietly, carrying one of the shovels with him, and found his way back to the opening.

He began pounding away with the point of the spade, and when he had been working for about five minutes, the noise aroused Boomer.

"Timmy, where are you?" he shouted.

"Over here," Timmy replied. "I couldn't sleep, so I decided I might as well get back to work."

"I guess I feel the same way."

Boomer joined Timmy with a shovel a few minutes later.

They worked carefully at the job of widening the opening. Finally Timmy's head and shoulders came out over a big, open space.

He reached back for the flashlight. The batteries were getting weaker all the time, and the bulb showed only a flicker of light. But there was enough of a glow to show them that they were on a rocky platform some distance up from the floor of a great cavern.

The silence and solemnity of the great cavern reminded Timmy of a church. He settled back in awe, and Boomer brushed up against his shoulder.

"What is it, Timmy? What do you see?"

"There's a big room here," Timmy replied in a husky whisper. "It's—well, it's almost like being in the cathedral in Capitol City."

He moved the flashlight around and realized one thing. They were high up on the wall of this new, rock-bound room—too high to be able to jump down or climb down, as they had been able to do in the main cave. The light Timmy was holding did not show them the floor, nor would it reach the high, arched roof of the cavern above them.

They did discover before long that the ledge widened out beyond the big opening they had made, and stretched off in both directions. Boomer crawled along it for a way. Timmy turned to start back into the connecting tunnel to get new batteries and a bulb for the flashlight.

While Boomer was moving along in the darkness there was a dry clatter as he stumbled into something. For a moment the cave was silent. Then Timmy heard a terrified cry.

"Timmy," Boomer screamed. "Timmy, don't leave me! Timmy, where are you?"

Timmy flicked on the weak flashlight. "What is it, Boomer?" he asked shakily. "What's wrong?"

Again there was silence. Then Boomer whispered hoarsely, "Come here, Timmy! And bring—bring—bring the light!" His teeth were chattering with fright.

Timmy Martin crawled toward his friend on his hands and knees.

"What is it, Boomer?"

"A dead man!" Boomer replied. "Back there on the ledge! Honest!" He pointed over his shoulder along his line of retreat.

Timmy almost choked. His grip on the flashlight loosened and it dropped to the rocky ledge beneath his feet. He scrambled for it, finally catching the metal cylinder before it rolled over the edge and into the gloom below.

He flicked the switch, and the cone of light picked up the trail in front of Boomer. There he saw, not a newly dead man as Boomer's words had suggested, but a skeleton. There were the remains of clothing wrapped around the bones—scraps of cloth and leather—and nearby was a bundle of arrows.

Timmy gulped.

"I guess he's dead, all right," he said. "But he's been dead a long, long, time."

"What do you think he was doing here?" Boomer asked when he got back his breath.

"Maybe he was one of the guardians of the Lost Cherokee Treasure, and he died protecting it," Timmy suggested. "The others left him here to look after it when he went up to the Happy Hunting Ground. Uncle Petrie said that Indians believed in symbols like that."

"Well, I wish they'd left him someplace else," Boomer

said vehemently. "Why did he have to be right here for me to fall over? He almost scared the daylights out of me."

Timmy tried to smile. "I guess they didn't know you'd be coming this way."

The problem of the Indian skeleton was pushed into the background by something else a few moments later. Suddenly a strange, whirring sound filled the huge room.

"What is it?" Boomer asked.

Timmy tried to light the ceiling of the cavern with the weak beam of the flashlight, but it would not reach. Then he realized that some of the noise was coming from close by, so he aimed the light in that direction. There, at the opening which they had widened, he saw a furry cloud moving past like some strange motion picture a little blurred and out of focus.

He whistled. "It's the bats—they're coming back! There's thousands of them! Look!"

"I'm looking, all right," Boomer managed in a whisper. "They're coming from a big hole up there in the ceiling. I think I can see some stars through it, and the beams of the moon. But that doesn't do us any good."

Timmy looked in the direction Boomer was pointing, and he, too, could see the sparkle of the stars and the gleam of the moonbeams.

"It's good to be able to see the sky again," Timmy said.

"Maybe good, maybe bad," Boomer replied.

Timmy was puzzled. "What do you mean by that?"

Boomer shivered. "We can see the way out that the bats used, but it's no way out for us. It's big enough, but how are we going to get up there? It must be at least fifty feet from where we're standing."

The two boys sat down on the ledge with their feet dangling into the darkness that filled the space below them. Timmy turned out the flashlight to save the batteries and the bulb.

"What do we do now?" Boomer asked.

"Think like a horse."

"A *horse?*" Boomer repeated. "What do you mean by that?"

Timmy laughed. "Last spring Mr. Thomas lost a horse. He looked all over for it and couldn't find it. When it was almost dark, Uncle Petrie came back with the horse. Mr.

Thomas asked Uncle Petrie how he found the horse and Uncle Petrie told him, 'I just figured out where I'd go if I was a horse and wanted to get myself lost. If you're hunting for a horse, you've got to think like a horse.' "

Boomer frowned as though he still didn't fully understand this comparison.

"Maybe Uncle Petrie was right," he said. "But I don't think any horse could get out of here through that hole in the roof."

"So we've got to think like an Indian," Timmy told him. "We know that they went in and out of here. All we have to find out is how they did it."

There was silence in the cave while the two boys considered the puzzle that faced them. Then Boomer said, "Well, out in the cliff dwellings of New Mexico and Arizona, they used ladders made of vines and poles, lashed together. Do you think they might have had something like that in here?"

Timmy thought this over for a while.

"They might have," he replied. "But we didn't find any poles or vines while we were coming in here, did we?"

Boomer shook his head. "They may be down in this big room below us, though. If we had some more light we could tell."

"Or maybe they're outside, and someone up there on top of Kingpin Mountain had to lower them down through that big hole to get out anyone who was trapped in here." Timmy took a gloomy view of the situation.

Boomer's brow furrowed as he thought a bit more about the problem. "Did you ever go into one of the upstairs rooms in the Calverton Hotel?" he asked.

"Went to a party on the second floor, once," Timmy recalled. Visions of cakes and ice cream filled his mind for a moment. "Why?" he asked.

"Did you ever see one of the rope ladders up there?" Boomer inquired. "They use them for fire escapes, I guess."

"Sure I saw 'em."

"Do you think the Indians might have had something like that?"

"They had ropes, all right," Timmy replied. "So there's no reason why they couldn't have rope ladders, too, if they needed them."

"Maybe we could make a rope and get down to the floor below here. Then we could look around and see if there were any of those Indian ladders you were talking about," Boomer suggested.

"How are we going to make a rope?" Timmy asked doubtfully.

"We can go back into the main cave and cut up one of our blankets and tie the pieces together. That ought to make a rope long enough to get down there."

They retraced their steps, selected a blanket, and began cutting it up to make a rope. The tying took a long while, but it was finally finished and the excited youngsters wound it into a ball and headed back into the inner chamber.

As they crawled along, Boomer asked, "Which one of us is going down the rope?"

"I'll go down," Timmy decided. "I'm the smallest, and you can pull me up if I get into trouble. I'd never be able to haul you up."

They came back to the spot where they had found the skeleton, and the two boys stood together, looking up at the opening which gave them a glimpse of the sky. Boomer sighed heavily.

"Tie it around your waist," Timmy said. "Then sit down and brace your feet against that rock there."

Boomer followed the suggestion, but it was obvious that he did not like this idea at all.

Timmy wrapped an arm around the blanket rope, then caught the lower end of it with his two legs. He climbed down slowly and kept talking to Boomer to report his progress and keep up the spirits of the older boy.

"Maybe there's an opening to the outside from down here on the floor," Timmy called when he was about halfway down. "Then we wouldn't have to worry about a ladder at all."

Moments later, something cold and clammy began gripping Timmy around the feet and legs. He pulled himself back up on the rope and called, "Pull, Boomer! Pull! Get me up out of here! Quick!"

"What's wrong?" Boomer shouted. "What's down there?"

"Pull me up quick!"

Even as Boomer was pulling in on the rope, Timmy was climbing it hand over hand. The way out of the cave was not going to be across the wide chamber below the ledge. He felt sure of that.

14 THE REAL INDIAN EXPERT

Lassie had almost succeeded in freeing herself of the entangling harness and the leash which had been holding her, when an angry Bill Gates discovered her in the grass. He blundered through the last ten yards, beating the brush with his walking stick.

The big collie tried to jump out of the way, but she was trapped by the pieces of leather that still held her. Gates struck her with the stick, then grabbed the tangled leash and began to beat her around the head and shoulders with it.

Any thoughts that Lassie might have had about going to the rescue of Timmy and Boomer were knocked out of her mind at that moment. She knew now that she would stay with her tormentor and make him pay for this attack he had made upon her.

Though she snapped and snarled furiously, Gates was finally able to free the harness and pack from the tangle of brush. He completed his repairs on the pack, checked to make sure that the money had not been disturbed in the flight through the woods, then dragged the collie back to the trail.

The escape might have seemed like a complete failure to whatever woods animals had been watching, but for Lassie it had accomplished at least one thing that might help her a lot in the future. She had succeeded in getting rid of the muzzle that had been fastened about her head.

Apparently Gates did not notice this, or if he did, he did not dare take time to look for it in the darkness. He might have felt, too, that now that he and Lassie were actually on their way, there was less need to confine the dog.

Lassie also realized, from the way that it slipped about, that the harness was much looser than it had been, and she knew that the leash was frayed from her gnawing and the run through the brush.

The eastern sky was brightening when they came down

off Kingpin Mountain. Lassie was on ground that was familiar to her. She had come this way with Sheriff Casey and Paul Martin and Timmy about a week before. Here was the end of the trail that led to the dirt road where the second getaway car had been hidden. The road would lead them out to the main highway from Lewiston.

But apparently Bill Gates had no intention of heading for Lewiston. He crossed the road, even though Lassie pulled back and tried to head down the route taken by the sheriff's cars when they had come to pick up the Martins and the posse.

"Come on, there!" he snarled. "We've got to get under cover before daylight!" He snapped the leash, wrenching Lassie's neck painfully.

The gallant collie turned and followed the bank robber. Soon they were beyond the road and following a winding trail that led up a hill through an old, neglected apple orchard. Lassie sensed that there were small animals in the tall grass, stirring for the new day and looking for their breakfast. Some of them scurried away as they realized there might be an enemy approaching.

Then the path opened into the overgrown yard of an obviously abandoned farm.

At the far end of the yard there was a weather-beaten house with gray, unpainted clapboard siding. At first glance it looked as if no one had been near the place for many years.

But a keen observer would have noticed several things. The once-sagging door had been rehung on new hinges, and there was a new lock holding it closed. There were several fresh boards on the wooden shutters that hung over two of the windows.

If no one was actually in the house, then someone had been there a short time ago to look after it. But Lassie knew that there was someone in the house. She knew that this was another enemy, because she recognized the scent as that of Sam Rowan, the man who had driven the getaway car from the Capitol City Farmers Bank.

The collie's instincts told her that Rowan was more friendly to her than Bill Gates had been. She knew in her canine mind that the driver of the car had prevented Gates from killing her when they were driving from Capitol

City to the abandoned quarry.

But would Sam Rowan help her again? There was no way the collie could tell.

Bill Gates became extremely cautious as he approached the house. He stopped behind one of two big oak trees that had once marked a gateway and pulled Lassie in close while he examined the whole area. There were no signs of any disturbance since he had left the place almost a week before. He bent slowly, picked up several pebbles, and began throwing them at one of the windows that had a shutter with new boards in it.

A muffled voice called out, "Who's there?"

Lassie recognized it immediately.

"Gates," her captor replied. "Open up there, but don't show yourself in the doorway!"

Several moments passed before the door opened a crack. Bill Gates took a last look all around, then grasped Lassie's collar and hurried across the yard to the old steps that led up to the door.

The trip from the oak tree to the door took not more than half a minute. Man and dog moved into a dark, dreary room, lighted only by narrow shafts of morning light that came through the cracks in the window shutters.

Lassie turned around quickly as Sam Rowan caught his breath.

"Bill, that dog! Where did you get her?"

"It was the kid's dog. I had to take her along to carry out my Indian expert act. And she's been a big help—carried half the money down the side of the mountain. I don't think she liked the job, but she did it anyway!" Bill Gates was a lot more lighthearted, now that he had finished the nighttime trip.

"But—this collie—isn't it the same one that tripped up Jack Crane in front of the bank? The one that followed you into the car?" Rowan gulped in fear. "The same one we—er—you drowned in the mine pit?"

Bill Gates snorted. "She didn't drown! I heard the Martins talking about it—and the sheriff too. The dog is a smart animal. She knows how to open and close door latches, and she let herself out of the car before it ever reached the edge of the pit and tumbled into the water . . . . Let's forget about it! We've got other things to do."

Rowan hurried forward to help with the unfastening of the knapsacks. The bandit looked at the stolen money and began to lick his lips as he thought about the things he would soon be able to buy.

"How about something to eat?" Bill Gates demanded. "I'm as hungry as a bear!"

"Coming right up," Rowan replied quickly. He went to one corner of the room where there was a wood stove and took a pot of coffee from the back, then began slicing some bacon into a pan. "I didn't know whether you'd make it this morning or not," he said.

"You got my signal the night before last from the top of Sentinel Rock, didn't you?"

"I saw that all right," Rowan agreed, "but I figured you'd be in here about midnight, or maybe two or three in the morning at the latest. When you didn't come then, I gave up."

Gates shrugged. Then he began wolfing down the food that his partner put in front of him.

Rowan set a plate of scraps in front of Lassie before he poured himself a cup of coffee.

"What do we do now, Bill?" he asked.

"Follow along with our plan," Gates replied, looking toward the stairway which led up to the second story. "Everything tight up there?"

"All quiet," Rowan replied mysteriously.

Lassie did not have to be told that there was someone upstairs; but the scent of the man was not one that she recognized, so she was not concerned about him at the moment.

"You mean we're ready to spring Jack?" Rowan asked.

"He'll be out of that jail in Capitol City by tomorrow night or the next night at the latest," Gates promised.

"How are we going to work it?" It was plain that Rowan was the softer of the two; he had to be reassured that everything was going to move smoothly before he could relax.

"There shouldn't be more than one or two jailers there," Gates explained. "The sheriff and the rest of the men will be out mule-driving!" Gates laughed. The picture was pleasing to him.

"Mule-driving?" Rowan repeated. "What are you talking about?"

"The sheriff and one of those newspaper men came up to the Indian cave to see me yesterday. They wanted to know how we were making out with the search for the Indian relics. They also asked about how we were going to get them down to Calverton and Capitol City."

Rowan grinned.

"You told them it might be done with mules, eh?"

"I don't remember now whether *I* suggested the mules, or whether it was the sheriff's idea. But they're coming up that mountain with mules tomorrow or the next day, so the coast will be clear down around the jail."

Rowan slapped his sides and laughed.

"Boy, will the sheriff be surprised when he gets up to that cave with the mules and finds out that you're gone—and the bank's money with you!"

"I guess he'll be a lot more surprised when he gets back to Capitol City and finds out that Jack Crane is gone too," Gates pointed out.

The two men were pleased with the way their plans were progressing. While Rowan was cleaning up the dirty dishes in an old tin dishpan alongside the hand pump in the sink, he asked another question that was running through his mind.

"What are we going to do about the professor upstairs—and the dog here?"

Bill Gates thought it over. "Maybe we could work out something with that outfit we're going to use to crack open the jail," he said softly.

He walked across the gloomy room to a pile of burlap bags in the corner, lifted them aside, and brought out a battered-looking suitcase. Inside was a large cigar box and in it there were a number of long, paper-wrapped objects which looked like Fourth of July Roman candles.

Lassie watched and knew what she was seeing. Paul and Uncle Petrie had used these same greasy-looking objects to blow up stumps on the Martin farm. They were sticks of dynamite.

Sam Rowan came up behind Gates and looked down into the suitcase over his shoulder. As Gates picked up a small bottle with yellowish-white liquid in it, Rowan leaped back and cried, "Don't fool around with that, Bill."

"Nitroglycerin is an old friend of mine," Gates replied.

"A little bit of this will go a long way—and anything it's pushing will go a long way too." He laughed.

Rowan paled. He ran his hand across his mouth as though he wanted to say something but did not want to make Gates angry while he was saying it. Finally he stammered, "If you're going to blow up the farmhouse, I want to be a long way from here when it happens!"

"So do I," Gates told him soberly. But he did not go on to explain what he planned to do. Instead he laid the little bottle back in the box and carefully closed the suitcase.

"Get together some breakfast for the professor," he ordered. "I'll take it up to him and see how he's making out. Then I'll catch up on my sleep for a couple of hours. You can head across the wood lot and make sure the car is in running order. We don't want anything to go wrong with this jail break."

Rowan dished up the last strips of bacon in the pan, poured a cup of black coffee into a heavy china cup, and handed them to Gates. Then he said, "Maybe I ought to take the dog with me too."

Lassie looked up at Rowan as though she thought it was

a good idea. But Bill Gates whirled around and shouted, "This dog isn't going anywhere! I figure we've been lucky to get in here without anyone seeing us. But if the collie gets away, there's no telling where she might turn up—and that could sure mean trouble. The dog stays right here with me!"

Rowan shrugged as though the matter was of small importance. He picked up a key case from the table and headed out the door. Gates locked it behind him.

Then Gates took Lassie by the collar and dragged her up the flight of stairs to the second floor. At the top of the stairs were two rooms, one on either side of the narrow stairway. Gates turned to the right and put a key into the lock of the door there. He kicked open the door and pushed Lassie into the room. Then he fumbled in his pocket with his free hand and brought out a pistol. He leveled this, edged the door back with his shoulder, and stepped forward.

On a brass bed across the room near a boarded-up window was the bound figure of a tall, sturdy-looking man. He was hunched up like a letter Z, but did not look especially uncomfortable. His eyes were open and he glared at Bill Gates defiantly as the robber came into the room.

"Good morning, Professor," Gates greeted him, pleasantly enough. "I hope you had a good night's sleep. Here's your breakfast."

Professor Harry Larkin swung himself to a sitting position and leaned his back against the head of the brass bed.

"I slept all right," he said. "But how long is this game going on?"

Gates smiled. "It's almost over now, I guess."

"That means you've gotten the stolen money, and you're ready to leave here?" The professor stated the question grimly. Then he looked at Lassie. His brows furrowed, and he frowned. "Where did the dog come from?"

"The Martin farm," Gates replied slowly. "You know, playing the part of Professor Larkin sure was fun. Folks treated me like I was the most important person in the world. You get a nice feeling about something like that."

The professor nodded. "Maybe that'll teach you that it's a good thing to go in for honest work—even if it's digging up Indian relics."

"You can't eat a nice feeling," Gates replied coldly. "I've got a big bundle of good American dollars right now, and I'm going to enjoy life. What have you got for all your digging?"

Professor Larkin looked at his captor thoughtfully. "Nothing *you'd* consider important, I guess."

"Eat up," Gates snorted, closing the conversation abruptly. "The dog will keep you company until we decide what we're going to do with you before we head out of here."

The bank robber turned and left the room. Lassie crossed to the bed and settled down beside the hobbled professor.

15 LASSIE TAKES THE BACK TRAIL

Daylight had come in quite different ways to Timmy and Boomer in the Indian cave and to Professor Larkin with Lassie in the farmhouse.

At the farm, the thin lines of light coming through the cracks in the shutters on the farmhouse windows finally broadened to a dull glow that brightened the whole house. But the only bit of daylight that Timmy and Boomer could see from the high shelf above the inner room in the Indian cave was the round circle of sky through which the bats had gone out to hunt, and by which they had come back into the cave's gloom to sleep through the day.

Several hours had passed since Boomer had been frightened almost out of his wits by Timmy's shout at the end of the blanket rope.

"What's down there, Timmy?" he had demanded as

his friend appeared over the rock ledge.

"Water!" Timmy had gasped. "Ice-cold water. I went into it up to my knees, and if I hadn't stopped when I did, I'd have gone in over my head."

"We should have known that," Boomer said. "Uncle Petrie told us that a lot of caves are caused by underground springs and underground rivers. We should have known that with all of these tunnels up here there would be some kind of spring around."

Timmy laughed, but he shivered too. "I found it, all right," he agreed.

The boys had dried Timmy's legs and bundled them up so that he would not catch cold; then they had decided to try to sleep again. This time they were so exhausted that they dropped off into a deep slumber.

Toward morning Timmy began repeating, "Lassie, Lassie, Lassie!" in his sleep. Boomer woke up when Timmy started stroking his hair as though he might be running his fingers through Lassie's silky ruff.

When Timmy awoke a short time later, Boomer told him that he had been talking in his sleep and they both began to worry about the big collie.

"I'm pretty sure Lassie can take care of herself, all right," Timmy said soberly. "But is she going to be able to bring anyone up here to help us?"

Boomer hoped so, but he didn't know any more than Timmy did. Finally he looked up at the opening in the dome of the inner cave and saw patches of daylight sky, wisps of white clouds moving by, and birds on the wing.

"Look, Timmy! The sun's up! We ought to be able to see what's down below us pretty soon."

Timmy nodded. They dangled their feet over the edge of the shelf. As the sun's angle shifted and the light came down into the cave, it caught the pool of water into which Timmy had almost fallen. The pond covered about half of the sloping floor and looked quite deep. But the objects on the other side of the inner room stirred a quick comment from Timmy.

"Boomer!" he shouted. "Look across there!"

The sun was shining on the bright colors of a small panel of cave pictures which were much clearer and more interesting than the ones in the main cave. Down on the stone floor below the pictures there were a number of boxes and old trunks, some of them bound in a metal that might be gold.

Timmy immediately decided that it *was* gold. But there was no way of telling; the boxes were as impossible to reach as if they were on the moon.

"Do you think that's it?" he cried.

"It?" Boomer repeated. He saw only the same kind of old trunks and boxes that he might find in the family attic or in the hayloft of the Bates barn.

"The Treasure!" Timmy explained quickly. "The Lost Cherokee Treasure!"

"Maybe," Boomer agreed slowly. "Maybe it is!" But his eyes had discovered something else as the slanting rays of the sun came farther into the cave room from the small opening above. There was a dark archway, about four feet high, behind the trunks and boxes. Boomer turned around and looked at the passage through which they had shoveled their way from the main cave. It was like a small archway too. He pointed quickly across the wide space of the inner room.

"Timmy, look over there! It's a way out! See it, behind those trunks and boxes?"

Timmy followed his friend's finger. "It looks like a way out, all right. But how are we going to get to it?"

The sunlight was climbing up the wall of the cave now from the surface of the pool of water and the area where stood the strange trunks and boxes. Finally it reached the ledge where the boys sat. They saw that the ledge, blocked here and there by rock falls which had come down from crevices above, extended all the way around the chamber. At some places it was only a few inches wide where the lower rock had broken off, but the boys thought they could make their way around it.

If they could do this, and take their blanket rope with them, they might be able to climb down onto the floor of the inner room and look over the new tunnel for a way of escape.

Timmy wanted to start right away, but Boomer was the more practical one.

"I'm getting hungry," he said. "I'm going back to the other cave and get the food and water. And maybe we'll

find some flashlight batteries too. We might need them, if we don't get out of here before tonight."

Timmy agreed and they hurried back to collect some of their belongings. When the job was done, the boys felt more cheerful than they had for several hours.

They had no trouble on the ledge, although there were times when Boomer's leather-soled shoes slipped and carried him dangerously close to the edge. Finally he took them off, tied the laces together, and hung the shoes around his neck. It was much easier walking on stocking feet. Timmy was wearing rubber-soled shoes, so he did not have much trouble.

Finally they were clear of the water. Then another question developed.

"Suppose we get down there and we can't get out through the tunnel," Timmy suggested. "How are we going to get back up here? If anyone comes looking for us, they'll be looking in the other cave."

"Anyone but Lassie," Boomer pointed out. "She'll know where we are, no matter where we go."

"Anyone but Lassie," Timmy agreed slowly. He looked

around and found a place where a point of rock jutted out from the wall. "I think we could tie the end of the blanket rope to that," he decided. "Then we could both climb up and down whenever we wanted to."

Boomer agreed and they fastened the rope. Timmy went down first, while his pal watched the anchor knots for signs of strain. Then Boomer took his turn. The rope stretched dangerously under Boomer's weight, but at last the two boys stood side by side on the stone floor.

"The Treasure!" Timmy grabbed Boomer's arm and they ran to the boxes. Trembling with excitement, they tried to force open one of the metal-bound covers.

"Aw, nuts! It's locked!" Boomer looked around in disgust. "They all are! We'll have to get some tools and stuff and come back!"

Timmy nodded disappointedly. But if they couldn't open the boxes, they could explore the tunnel that might lead to freedom. He got down on his hands and knees and moved forward slowly through the archway. Then he wrinkled his nose as an unpleasant odor stirred his sense of smell. It was a heavy, musty odor.

"It smells like something died in here," he said to Boomer over his shoulder.

Boomer shivered. Then he sniffed. He backed into the Indian chamber and stood up.

"I've smelled that before—I know what it is!" he exclaimed. "Timmy, we've got to go back!"

"Why?"

"The smell!" Boomer gasped. "I've smelled it at the Capitol City zoo. In the bear pit!"

"Bear pit?" Timmy repeated, half in question. "You mean there might be bears at the other end of this tunnel? Well, wouldn't they make some kind of noise, if they were there?"

"If it's a mother bear and her cubs, they're probably out hunting for food right now. The cubs would be three or four months old, and the mother would be real mean if anyone came close." Boomer was slapping his hands together as though they were cold.

"Well," Timmy said, "if the bears are out hunting, I should think this would be the best time for us to try and get through the den and out into the open air."

"Not me!" Boomer declared quickly. "We don't know when the bears might be coming back."

Timmy studied his friend, undecided. Then he turned around and moved toward the blanket rope.

"You can do as you like," Timmy said briskly. "I'm going to get my shovel and get out through that tunnel."

But as he was crossing the stone floor, a long, low, snarl came from the other end of the tunnel. Boomer ran past Timmy and stumbled to the floor.

"See—they're back already!" he stammered. "We're not going to—to get out—that—way!"

Back in the farmhouse, Lassie watched while Professor Larkin ate his breakfast and juggled the cup of coffee with bounds hands. Larkin looked at the dog, then dropped his hands onto the dog's head.

"You must be Lassie. Miss Crane wrote about you in the letter she sent to Washington. But how did you get mixed up with these robbers?"

Lassie barked as though she would like to explain things to the professor but did not know how to do it. The collie sniffed around the ropes which bound the professor's arms and feet and fastened his body to the brass bed. She worried several of the knots with her teeth.

Suddenly there was a sound on the stairs.

"Down, Lassie!" the professor commanded. "Get away, girl!"

Bill Gates unlocked the door and strode across the room. He took the plate and cup from the professor without speaking and started back toward the door.

"When are you going to turn us loose?" the professor demanded.

"Turn you loose?" Gates turned. "Who said anything about turning you loose? You'd go running to the police as soon as you got a chance. We can't have you doing that."

"But if you leave us here, we're likely to starve to death," Professor Larkin pointed out. "This farm is a long way from the road—no one would come past here from one end of the week to the other."

Gates chuckled. "This looks like good deer-hunting country," he commented. "Someone ought to be coming around about the first of November."

"First of November?" Professor Larkin groaned. "But this is only the middle of July!"

"Not too far from the Fourth for a little fireworks," the bank robber said slyly. "If this farmhouse happened to go up with a big boom, the neighbors might think that some of the local kids were playing with firecrackers or something like that. I don't think they'd worry too much about it, do you?"

Professor Larkin went pale and Lassie snarled. Bill Gates turned on his heel and headed for the door. Just before he locked it behind him, he looked back at his prisoners with a smile.

"You'll really go out in a blaze of glory, won't you?" he said softly.

Then the Indian expert and the dog were left alone. Lassie lifted her forepaws to the edge of the bed and went at the knots in Professor Larkin's ropes with new speed and determination.

As the ropes began to loosen, Larkin pulled on them, and gradually they came apart. When the professor was able to sit up and shake the loose bonds from around his body, he turned back to Lassie and worked diligently on the leather straps and remains of the harness which still interfered with her complete freedom of movement.

The man patted Lassie on the forehead. "Lassie, girl, I think we're ready to do something about this whole business."

The collie began to bark softly, but Larkin closed her jaws and shook his finger as though any sound might be dangerous.

The tight bonds had cut off the Indian expert's circulation and almost paralyzed his arms and legs. Now he was able to exercise and rub the blood back into these extremities and feel new life in them.

"Wish I had a weapon that might give me a little chance against a gun—or a stick of dynamite," Larkin whispered. He walked around the room, searching for something to use as a weapon. But the two bank robbers had been careful in checking Larkin's prison. No object in the bedroom was tough enough or big enough to make a good club.

Finally the professor settled down on the edge of the

bed. He bent over, took off one of his shoes, and removed the sock. He held it in his hand for several moments, then turned to the nearest high post of the brass bed.

There was a heavy metal ball on top of the post. After a bit of twisting Larkin managed to start it turning on its screw base, and moments later it came off. He dropped it into the sock, tied a knot to hold it in place, and swung the sock experimentally. It made a good weapon.

"This ought to do it, Lassie," he told the collie.

Lassie whimpered. She had been watching him as he worked, wondering whether the men she knew were always sure of what they were doing.

Hours had passed since breakfast. Finally, early in the afternoon, the man and the dog heard footsteps on the stairs. This time they could tell that both men were coming up to see them.

"Get ready, Lassie!" Larkin said in a hoarse whisper.

The collie settled down at the foot of the bed. The fact that she had been freed of all her bonds would not be seen immediately. Larkin had dropped back on the bed, concealing his brass-ball club beside his body. The ropes were draped over his arms and legs so they would look secure at a careless glance.

A sense of excitement stirred Lassie. Then there was a hand on the doorknob and a moment later Gates and Rowan stepped into the room.

"You're worrying so much about the dog," Gates sneered. "Keep an eye on him while I check the professor."

Rowan nodded and moved toward the foot of the bed where Lassie was crouched, ready. Bill Gates strode up, looked down casually at Harry Larkin, then bent over to check his bonds.

"Let's get them, Lassie!"

As Larkin flung himself erect and snatched up the sock club, Lassie leaped away from the foot of the bed. Gates dropped his hand to his coat pocket, fumbling belatedly for his gun.

"Shoot her!" he shouted. "Shoot the dog!"

Lassie realized the danger of the order and she jumped up into Sam Rowan's arms. He was trying to reach for his own gun in a shoulder holster, but the collie grabbed his wrist and hung on with her teeth. She began to shake him furiously as she might shake a rat.

"Help me, Bill! Help me! She's killing me!"

But Gates was in no shape to help anyone but himself—and he was having a desperate fight to do that.

16 SEARCH FOR THE LOST BOYS

When Bill Gates discovered that Professor Larkin was untied, he was more startled than concerned. He knew they had searched the room carefully and had left no loose weapons lying around. Therefore it was a surprised bandit who felt the first impact of the brass-ball club.

Harry Larkin struck him on the wrist first, and the pistol dropped to the floor. Then he raised the weapon to slam Gates over the head. The bank robber turned to run, and the descending ball struck him at the base of the brain.

Bill Gates fell forward with a crash. Professor Larkin stared at him, stunned at the thought that he might have killed the man. A glance showed him that Lassie was giving a good account of herself with the other bandit and needed no immediate help. He knelt quickly to check Gates's pulse and breathing, and found, to his very great relief, that the bandit was alive, though unconscious.

Lassie's attack on Sam Rowan was a fierce one, and the bandit, who did not have anything like the killer instinct of his partner, dropped his gun and tried to jump away from the dog. The collie held her grip on Rowan's wrist, however, and the weight of the animal was enough to turn Sam sideward and send him staggering against the foot-board of the bed.

Rowan shouted for help, but then he saw Gates toppling to the floor in front of the professor. He turned and, dragging Lassie behind him, tried to run for the door.

Harry Larkin picked up Gates's gun. "I wouldn't do that if I were you, Rowan," he said steadily.

Sam turned around, and Professor Larkin smiled grimly. "I guess you can let go now, Lassie."

At the friendly voice, the collie released her grip and moved back a few paces toward Larkin where she stood calmly but alertly waiting for the next step in this drama.

Professor Larkin gestured with the gun. "Come over here, Sam. I have a job for you."

Rowan came.

"Lift Gates up on the bed. Then take those ropes you used on me and see how well you can tie up your partner."

Rowan might have wanted to protest, but he saw that it would gain him nothing. He began working with the ropes. When he had used about half of them, Larkin ordered him to stop.

"That'll do for him. Now sit down beside him on the bed and I'll check your job on Gates, then tie you up."

Rowan smiled slightly, as if this was a chance he had been waiting for. But before he could make a move, Professor Larkin patted Lassie on the head and said, "You keep an eye on him, Lassie, girl!"

The professor had put the club in one pocket and now he stuffed Gates's gun into the other. Lassie came up on her hindquarters and stiffened her forelegs as she faced Rowan.

Larkin went over the ropes on Bill Gates very carefully, tightening some of the knots here and there, then turned his attention to Rowan. It did not take him long to finish the tying job.

"Not bad," he said finally. "I think these ropes ought

to hold you fellows while I go looking for help. What do you think, Lassie? Can you stand guard?"

Lassie barked her agreement, then moved back out of reach of the men on the bed and took up a position where she could watch both of them.

Professor Larkin came over to the collie and patted her on the head.

"I'm sure you'll look after things while I'm gone. I don't think you have any more reason to like these fellows than I have, eh?"

Lassie replied with short, sharp yips, and Larkin smiled. He picked up Rowan's gun and left the room.

Lassie whined a bit until she heard him cross the hallway below and close the front door behind him. Then she turned back to Gates and Rowan and settled down to wait.

Gates was still unconscious and Rowan was watching the dog nervously. When it became apparent that she was not going to turn wolf on him, he tried to talk to her. Lassie listened to the soft words but did not move from her guard position.

At last Bill Gates began to stir. His eyes opened and he

focused them with difficulty on Rowan who lay close beside him.

"What's happening here?" he muttered.

"The dog and that crazy professor!" Sam Rowan shouted. "We weren't going to have any more trouble with them! That's what you said!"

Gates was in no mood to argue. He looked about him with eyes that were still hazy.

"Where is he?" he asked. "What happened to our guns?"

"He's gone for the sheriff, I guess, and he's taken the guns with him," Rowan replied.

Gates shook his head to clear it. "Don't worry," he said quickly. "We'll be long gone by the time they get back here. I never saw any ropes I couldn't shake out of. Come on over here and give me a hand."

Lassie snarled then and began to move in slowly.

"Not me," Rowan declared quickly. "I'm not going to buck that she-dog again."

"She can't hurt you."

Rowan exhibited his bound hands. The marks of Lassie's teeth were still visible on his wrist.

"This doesn't look like it, does it?" he demanded.

Bill Gates snorted, then rolled over cautiously and tried loosening his own bonds. But Lassie was determined not to permit that either. She leaped onto his legs and swung her head at his straining hands.

Gates reared back and managed to throw Lassie aside. But his bound hands and legs were a disadvantage to him. Rowan laughed bitterly at his partner's struggles, but while Lassie was engaged with Gates he thought he saw a chance to get free from his own bonds. He backed up against the nailed shutters covering the windows of the farmhouse, and got the strands of rope over one of the nailheads.

The bandit sawed on the ropes gingerly, keeping his eyes on Lassie and Gates. Gates was snarling and swinging at the dog, knocking her aside now and then with his clenched fists. Gradually the loops around his wrists began to loosen as he worked his fists from side to side.

"What are you doing, Sam?" he gasped.

"Trying to get loose, of course."

"Take care of this dog for a while," Gates ordered. "I'll be free in no time."

Rowan threw his weight across Lassie's back and almost pinned her to the bed. But the muscular dog wriggled free and rolled down onto the floor. Rowan was tossed to one side in spite of himself. Frantically he tugged at the frayed cords on his wrists, twisting away from Lassie's attack, but the collie threw herself at his legs and toppled him to the carpet.

This time it was Gates who laughed.

"You're not going to get very far that way," he jeered.

Lassie backed off and kept her distance, while the two men lay quietly, facing her, and planning their next move. The collie stirred as the bandits finally moved, very slowly, into a position where they were seated back to back. Sam Rowan fumbled with the loosened cords on Gates's wrist. When he had forced these free, the bandit was able to complete the weakening of Rowan's cords which had already been frayed on the window nail.

The men worked cautiously, with as little movement as possible. But eventually they had to bring their hands out from behind their backs and begin working at the bonds on their feet. Instantly Lassie darted toward Sam

Rowan and struck him in the chest, throwing him over backward. In the meantime, however, Bill Gates wriggled free, leaped to his feet, and aimed a kick at Lassie's forehead. She hurtled away from him.

"Come on, Sam!" Gates shouted.

Rowan climbed erect, kicked the ropes loose from his legs, and followed his partner toward the bedroom door. But Lassie was close behind them. The two men and the dog reached the top of the stairs at almost the same moment. Lassie slammed into Gates's chest as he whirled around to fend her off. The bandit lost his balance, fell back against Rowan who was tottering at the top of the stairs, and then both men rolled backward down toward the first floor.

Rowan landed at the bottom of the stairway with a thud that shook the house. Gates fell on top of him. Lassie followed them down, and when Gates tried to get up, she settled her weight on his fallen figure and snarled warningly.

Then she started to bark. There was triumph in the sound, and as if in answer, a car drove into the farmyard outside. The sound of voices came to the dog, and the two men who were trying to thrust the collie aside suddenly gave up. They knew that the game was over.

Lassie had recognized the voices of Professor Larkin, Sheriff Bert Casey, and Paul Martin. The heavy tramp of boots on the little porch outside and the banging open of the door marked the approach of the three men. Then they were in the room.

Paul caught the tableau at the foot of the stairs.

"Lassie, girl! Lassie!" he shouted. "What's going on here?"

Lassie ran toward her master as Sheriff Casey hurried forward, gun drawn. He handcuffed the two men together and pulled them to a standing position.

Professor Larkin was beaming. He knelt beside the dog and began roughing up her brown and white coat. Paul took a quick look at the two bandits to make sure that the sheriff would have no trouble with them; then he turned to Lassie and knelt on her other side.

"Lassie, Lassie! Where are they? Where are Timmy and Boomer?"

Lassie barked once or twice and started for the doorway.

She seemed ready and anxious to lead Paul and the others to the lost boys.

Paul jumped up to follow, but Sheriff Casey hesitated. He was willing to depend upon the collie, but at the same time he wanted to get what information he could from Bill Gates—Gates whom he had last seen as the bogus Professor Larkin, with the boys at the cave.

He took the bank robber by the lapels of his coat and shook him.

"Where are they, Gates?" he demanded. "Where did you leave them?"

Gates was stubbornly silent.

"Rowan is the weak one," said Professor Larkin. "Maybe he'll tell us."

Sheriff Casey turned to the other bandit. "What about it? Where are they?"

Rowan looked at Gates and then at his captors. His face was gray.

"They're in the cave," he said finally. "Gates left them there—they had plenty of food and water."

Lassie was jumping against the sheriff's chest in a frenzy

of impatience at this delay. She knew where Timmy and Boomer were, and she wanted to take the men to them without any more delay.

"Hold on, old girl," Sheriff Casey told the collie. "We'll be right with you."

He and Professor Larkin herded the two robbers out the front door, with Lassie running ahead. Two possemen were waiting in the car.

"Any news about the boys?" asked the man at the wheel.

"Rowan says they're still in the cave—and safe enough with plenty of food and water."

The posseman shook his head. "You'd better pick up Al Bronson on the radio, Sheriff," he said. "He's up on the mountain with the men you sent to hunt for the boys at the cave."

Bert Casey nodded and picked up his microphone.

"Casey calling B-12. Come in, B-12. Casey calling B-12. Come in, B-12."

B-12 was the call number of the walkie-talkie radio the Capitol City *News-Telegram* reporter had with him on Kingpin Mountain.

Moments later the reply came back, loud and clear: "B-12 calling Casey. Come in, Casey!"

"We have the bank robbers, B-12. How are you making out with the missing boys?"

"B-12 to Casey. No news on the boys. We've been to the cave and cleared away the rocks from the opening. The boys aren't there."

Sheriff Casey lowered the mike slowly. Then he snapped it up to his mouth again.

"Casey to B-12. Keep looking around that cave, B-12. We'll be getting up there as soon as we can. Over and out."

Casey returned the microphone to its holder on the car's dashboard and turned around to face Gates.

"Those kids are gone, Gates. And if they're not found pretty quick, you're in big trouble."

Paul Martin's face was white. He tried to say something, but the words would not come. Finally he turned back to Lassie.

"Where are they, Lassie? Where are they?" he asked pleadingly.

Professor Larkin studied the worried father and the

excited dog. "What are you going to do now, Sheriff?" he asked.

"I was going to take the long way around the mountain through Lewiston with the prisoners," Casey replied. "I'd like to make sure they're safe in jail in Capitol City, and I'd like to get the stolen money back to the bank. It'll have to be held in escrow as evidence, but I want it to be somewhere safe."

Professor Larkin nodded his understanding. "Couldn't you send the money and the prisoners with the deputies in the car, while we follow Lassie up the mountain from this side? I'm sure she could lead us there, and I'll bet she can find the boys too."

Lassie barked to add her voice to the plea.

Sheriff Casey looked from the dog to the silent Paul Martin. "What do you think, Paul?" he asked. "You're the one most concerned."

"I believe Lassie can find Timmy," Paul replied soberly. "She can if anyone—I'm sure Lassie can do it."

Sheriff Casey reached a decision. He turned to the possemen. "Go inside and get the money—the bags are in the corner next to the stairs. Take it to Bob Hanson at the Farmers Bank. Tell him to put it in the county's box for the time being. He'll understand."

The posseman nodded, then turned a shotgun in the direction of the prisoners.

"How about them?"

"They'll be coming with us," Casey decided. "If this Gates fellow has done anything to Timmy or Boomer, I'll want to have him close enough to lay my hands on him when we find out about it."

Lassie whined and Professor Larkin shuddered. Casey gestured to the collie.

"Okay, Lassie, let's go!"

The dog barked eagerly and started away from the farmhouse. She was so excited that many times she got far ahead of the sheriff, the professor, Paul, and the prisoners, and she had to circle back to make sure they were still coming along. At first, when she ran out of sight, Sheriff Casey called to her, but soon he realized that she would not leave them behind.

The trip up Kingpin Mountain took about an hour and

a half. When they were still a quarter of a mile from the Indian caves, it was possible to glimpse the open area around Sentinel Rock, and Lassie and her companions could see men searching. The climbers hastened their steps, realizing that the boys had not yet been found.

Finally Lassie bounded out into the clearing, barking loudly. Paul was only a few steps behind her, and he immediately spotted Uncle Petrie and Al Bronson.

Lassie headed for the older man, and Uncle Petrie bent down to pet her.

"Golly," the old man said, "Lassie is sure a sight for sore eyes! I've got a hunch we're going to wind up this hunt right here and now. Go get them, Lassie! Find Timmy and Boomer!"

The collie moved toward the opening of the outer cave near where Bill Gates had dug up the stolen money. The landslide had been cleared away. Al Bronson and some of the possemen were standing there, and the expressions on their faces showed that they were discouraged. Lassie sniffed around them, then moved into the cave. Bronson followed.

"You're pretty smart, Lassie, but you're wrong this time,"

he said. "They're not in there. We've searched the place from top to bottom. They have been there, because there are a lot of new Indian relics I didn't see when I was here the last time, but the boys aren't in the cave."

Lassie snorted as though humans sometimes made her very unhappy. Then she hurried down the passage into the main cave.

Behind, Professor Harry Larkin asked quickly, "Did you say new Indian relics? Where are they?"

Bronson told him, and the Indian expert immediately lighted a lantern and followed Lassie into the cave. Uncle Petrie went along behind him. What a difference, he thought, between the real Professor Larkin and the false one! His work was so important to the professor that he could not put it out of his mind, even at a time like this.

Paul was on Uncle Petrie's heels as they made their way into the cavern. Lassie went to the spot where Timmy had dropped the bowl the day before. She sniffed at the Indian treasures, then lifted her muzzle and tried the air all about her.

She went over to a pile of bedding near the pottery and

began rooting among the blankets. Then she barked and ran toward the ledge in the rear of the cave.

Paul Martin felt a surge of hope. He hurried along after her calling, "Where are they, Lassie? Where are they?"

The ledge on which the boys had found the new Indian discoveries, and which had served as the route to the exit of the bats, was too high for Lassie to reach by jumping. She reached the sharply sloping wall and pawed her way up until she was standing erect and stretching as far as she could.

"Are they up there, Lassie, girl?"

Lassie barked sharply. Paul took hold of the dog's hindquarters and lifted her up to the ledge. She rested for a moment, then moved along gingerly, sniffing the ground before her.

Al Bronson shook his head. "We checked that ledge. It runs into a dead end."

But Lassie wasn't taking the word of anyone. She hurried on to an apparently blank wall, sniffed at it again, and picked up the strong scent of Timmy and Boomer. She barked furiously.

Paul turned to the Indian expert. "Do you think there might be another way out of here? Some way that might lead into one of the other caves?"

Professor Larkin looked up from his examination of the relics. "Most Indians would have two or three exits from a cave like this," he replied. "They'd probably lead into the other caves around here, or up through the roof—the Indians were great for roof openings. It served two purposes to have one. They could get out that way, and it was an escape vent for the smoke from their fires."

"We searched the other caves," Al Bronson pointed out. "The only one which looked as though it might lead into the larger cave was occupied." Bronson hesitated.

"Occupied?" Paul broke in. "By whom?"

"It would be better to say by what," Bronson replied. "It was being used as a den by a mother bear and two cubs. I don't know whether the big bruin was living there, too, or not. But they were home when we looked in, and they didn't like the idea of our moving in on them."

Paul Martin shuddered.

"Suppose the boys found that way out, and dug their

way into the bears' den," he said. "They might be in there now!"

Lassie was only mildly interested in all this exchange among the men who were working with her. She had her own instincts to guide her and she was convinced of one thing. Timmy and Boomer were alive and well. They were only a few feet away, behind that blank wall. She must get to them.

She barked loudly again.

When she stopped for breath this time, the dog and the men around her suddenly stiffened. For a familiar voice was calling, "Lassie! Lassie, is that you?"

Paul Martin gulped. "It's him!" he gasped. "It's Timmy—he's all right!" He ran forward and struck the wall with his bare hands. "Timmy!" he shouted. "Where are you?"

17 THE CHEROKEE TREASURE

Timmy sounded as though he was laughing and crying at the same time.

"We're in a big room on the other side of the cave wall," he shouted. "There's a passage from the ledge on the north side of the main cave. We walled it up again. But we'll start breaking through from this side."

"Are you all right, Timmy?" Uncle Petrie called hoarsely.

"I'm all right," Timmy replied, "and so is Boomer."

Lassie was working with her forepaws at the stones blocking the ledge passage, but she was not making very much progress. Paul and Al Bronson climbed up to help the dog, and Professor Larkin hurried forward.

"Don't move anything yet! Take it easy!"

Sheriff Casey, Paul, Uncle Petrie, and the others looked

at the Indian expert in surprise.

"The Indians walled up that passage in their own special way," Larkin explained. "I'm not sure how much damage the boys did getting through there. But there's a whole story here in these pictographs all around the walls of the outer cave. We don't want to destroy anything, now that we've found something this interesting."

"But the boys!" Paul insisted. "They must be frantic by this time. We've got to get to them!"

Professor Larkin shook his head. "They told you they were all right," he pointed out. "And now that they know that you and Lassie are here, I'm sure they'll be able to wait a little while for you to reach them. Judging from the letter I received from your Miss Lottie Crane, Timmy and Boomer are almost as interested in this Indian business as I am. After all the suffering they have gone through up to now, I don't think they'd want you to spoil it—do you?"

Neither Paul nor Uncle Petrie could debate the point. Paul cupped his hands and called, "Take it easy, boys! We'll be getting in there as soon as we can."

Timmy and Boomer shouted a reply, and Lassie added

her impatient barks to the sounds in the caves.

Convinced that the men would not hurry matters, Professor Larkin went back to where the searchers had left their packs and returned with a mining pick and some other more delicate tools. He cleared a place below the ledge and set out a blanket very carefully. Then he began breaking away the wall and putting the pieces on the blanket in the same order in which he took them out.

The manner in which he worked impressed the men. He seemed to know just where the wall would give, and the pieces of limestone that came out looked as though they might have been roughhewn by the Indians themselves.

The sounds of shoveling came from the other side of the opening. Professor Larkin listened for a moment, then called, "Let me do the digging, boys. Lay aside your shovels. I can see where you've walled up the tunnel, and we'll be through to you in no time."

The clatter from the other side stopped. Everyone was taking orders from the professor except Lassie. She kept close enough to Larkin to be breathing on his cheek most of the time, and the Indian expert had to push her gently aside several times. As soon as the first break-through was made into the cave, and before it was wide enough for a human, Lassie wriggled past the professor and into the inner cave.

Timmy and Boomer were crouched on either side of the opening. They fell upon the big collie as though they had never expected to see her again.

"Lassie! Lassie! You're here! We thought the robbers might have killed you."

Professor Larkin had his head and shoulders through the opening by this time. Timmy and Boomer turned their attention from the collie and looked up at him. Then they pushed back along the ledge.

"Who are you?" Timmy cried. "What are you doing here? Where's my dad and Uncle Petrie?"

Timmy was choking back tears. Boomer held the flashlight as though it were a weapon and he intended to defend them from the professor with it.

Larkin studied the two bedraggled-looking boys. Their faces were dirty and tear-streaked, their clothes torn. "I'm the real Professor Larkin you've been waiting for," he explained softly "I've come out here from Washington to help you with your Indian discoveries. We'll talk about the whole thing when we get a little more time . . . . So you were worried about the bank robbers killing Lassie, eh?"

"Yes—yes, sir, Professor," Timmy stammered.

Professor Larkin laughed. "There was a time there, about two hours back, when I thought maybe Lassie might be going to kill one of the robbers."

"How was that?" Timmy asked excitedly.

"They were holding me a prisoner over in a farmhouse, near Lewiston," the professor explained. "One of them—the man you knew as Professor Larkin—brought Lassie there. She was turned into the room where I was being kept, and she immediately helped me to get rid of my ropes. We took care of those bank robbers then in jig time."

"Good old Lassie!" Timmy cried. He hugged the collie and rubbed her ears.

Then the professor climbed through the opening to join the boys on the ledge, and the other members of the search party followed.

"Timmy!" Paul Martin embraced his son, hardly able

to believe that the hours of uncertainty were over.

Uncle Petrie threw an arm around Boomer's shoulder. "You fellows sure had a lot of excitement up here, didn't you?" he commented.

"Y-Yeah!" Boomer swallowed. "I was half scared to death, Uncle Petrie, and so was Timmy."

"But we're not scared now," Timmy broke in.

"Of course you aren't," his dad agreed. "But I'll bet your mom is pretty scared by now. And Boomer's folks too. I think we ought to head back right away and tell them you're all right."

Timmy looked up at his father. Then he turned to Professor Larkin.

"Are you going right back to the farm, Professor?" he asked slowly.

"Not right away," the professor replied. "Maybe sometime this afternoon."

Timmy didn't know what to do. But Al Bronson, an understanding man if there ever was one, took care of the problem very nicely.

"Sheriff," he said, "we left one of your cars in the Martin

farmyard. Do you think the man on duty there would have his radio turned on?"

"He should have," Sheriff Casey replied.

"Then I'll call him on my walkie-talkie. He can give Ruth the good word that Timmy and Boomer are safe and that the big search for the Lost Cherokee Treasure is going into high gear." He started back to the opening in the wall. "I'll do it right now."

Paul smiled. Timmy relaxed.

"That ought to take care of everything!" Uncle Petrie exclaimed. "I've got a hunch that Professor Larkin and the boys will find what they're after in a hurry, anyway. After all, they'd like to get a good night's sleep in a soft bed, like the rest of us. They're not going to stay up here any longer than they have to right now."

Timmy's head bobbed in agreement. "There's some big chests and boxes down there." He pointed into the pit below. "We couldn't open them, but I'm sure they must be real valuable."

Professor Larkin could not hide his excitement. Carefully he made his way around the ledge to where the blanket rope was still fastened to the rock pinnacle, and sliding down this he came to the floor of the chamber at the edge of the wide, deep pool of water. The boys followed him, and after Lassie had been lowered in a sling the possemen were close behind. Al Bronson returned to the inner cave as the last man reached the floor. He located them easily in the light of the lanterns and the hazy sunlight coming through the hole in the ceiling.

Timmy and Boomer led the way to the chests and boxes, with Lassie strutting along beside them as though she considered herself a full partner in anything they had found. Professor Larkin studied the boxes from all angles for a while. Then he opened one of them carefully with one end of his mining pick and stared down at the contents.

"Oh, boy!" shouted Timmy. "Look at that!"

They all crowded around the box.

"I was right!" Uncle Petrie said breathlessly. "It sure didn't take you very long to find what you were looking for."

Lassie glanced at the golden bowls and cups, the head-dresses set with jewels. She didn't know why people became so excited over shining metal and colored glass.

"Well, there's not much doubt that you boys have found it," Professor Larkin declared. "This looks as though it's the Lost Cherokee Treasure all right. And what's more, in looking around this cave it seems to me that the men who were guarding it spent a good deal of time here, making sure that it was protected from the weather and their enemies. They were here long enough to make this a real Indian ceremonial room."

Al Bronson was listening intently and making notes on the remarks of the Indian expert.

"I thought these Indian ceremonial rooms were decorated with wall paintings and hangings and things of that kind," he said.

"They usually were," Professor Larkin agreed. "And I think this one is decorated too."

Timmy and Boomer looked at him, not understanding him at all. The walls around them looked pretty dull and unexciting except for the small picture-panel they had seen that morning. They were gray and brown, and some of the rock showed damp spots where rain or snow had come in through the opening in the roof and trickled down across the inside.

Professor Larkin smiled at the puzzled boys.

"The American Indians were experts in all kinds of disguise. They knew how to conceal themselves in the midst of their enemies. They could move along as quietly as a snake in the dust. And they could communicate with sounds that were like the gobble of a turkey or the bark of a dog, or the howl of a wolf. They had their gaily decorated ceremonial room while they were living here away from their enemies. But when they had to leave they tried to conceal it."

To make his explanation more clear, Professor Larkin took a wooden hammer from his pocket and approached one section of the wall which looked as though it were covered with brown stucco. He tapped the head of the hammer against the surface of the wall, and a large area of the stone broke away. It was a thin covering like plaster and it crumbled when it struck the rocky floor. Beneath it the boys and the men could see bright colors.

Professor Larkin worked carefully, and finally an area

about five feet square was uncovered. The painting showed Indians in some kind of religious ceremony. The professor held up his lantern to bring out the colors and light the painting.

"The whole room should be covered with figures like these. There's not much doubt that we've found what we are looking for. Now we must work carefully to preserve it."

For the next hour the little group watched with interest, helping where they could as Professor Larkin uncovered more of the painted wall. After a while, Timmy discovered he was shivering. He looked around and saw in the dim light that his father and Boomer and all the others were looking cold and tired. Even Lassie stood with her head low, revealing the effects of the day's adventures.

Finally Timmy and Boomer sat down on a rock and Uncle Petrie joined them. Lassie came over and laid her head in Timmy's lap. The boy put his hand on her head.

"You sure had us scared for a while, Timmy," Uncle Petrie said. "Why didn't you let us know where you were? Couldn't you hear us working around in the other cave?"

Timmy looked at Boomer and they both smiled tired smiles.

"We could hear you all right," Timmy said, "but we thought it might be Professor Larkin—or whatever his real name was—coming back. We didn't want to let him know where we were, so we blocked up the opening. Then we just sat still and kept quiet until we heard Lassie barking. We knew she might have the pretend-professor with her, but we decided to take a chance and yell. We *couldn't* keep quiet any longer."

Uncle Petrie nodded. He looked in the direction of Professor Larkin, who was moving about the cave, examining everything and making notes like a man in a dream.

"Do you think you're going to enjoy working with him more than you did with Bill Gates?" Uncle Petrie asked slyly.

"Oh, boy, I sure do!" Timmy replied excitedly. "He *acts* like a real Indian expert. That other man didn't act like he knew what he was doing most of the time. At least he didn't know about Indian arrows and tomahawks and spears and things like that."

Sheriff Casey was standing behind the boys and Uncle Petrie, and he laughed at the comment.

"He didn't even make a good bank robber," the sheriff pointed out.

Then Casey went back to take charge of Bill Gates and Sam Rowan, who had been left in the main cave with a guard. Paul and Uncle Petrie were deciding what to do next, when Professor Larkin came over to them.

"I think I'd like to head for your farm now, Mr. Martin," he said. "But do you think the sheriff would leave someone here to look after things for a while? I'll have funds to defray any expenses."

"I'm sure he will," Paul agreed. "Let's go ask him before he gets away from us."

They all climbed back up the blanket rope in a hurry. No one realized that they were missing part of the expedition until Lassie whined in the semidarkness of the inner chamber. Then Uncle Petrie and Timmy looked down the rope and laughed. Lassie couldn't climb the rope. Paul slid back down and again made a sling at the end of the rope and settled Lassie into it. The collie wriggled for several moments, but when Uncle Petrie and the boys lifted her to the ledge, she seemed to enjoy the trip.

Outside of the main cave the group found Sheriff Casey telling Gates and Rowan how lucky they were that the boys had been found safe and sound. As the possemen and Al Bronson led the bandits down the trail toward the Martin farm and Calverton, the professor explained his problem to the sheriff.

"Glad to help you out, Professor," he said. "We'll keep a guard right here. But do you think this is really the Lost Cherokee Treasure?"

Professor Larkin looked around at the boys and their elders and then down at the loyal Lassie.

"I have a list of the things that were taken from the Great Smokies when the Cherokees left for Oklahoma," he said. "I'll be able to check it in due course. But I do think we may have found the Lost Cherokee Treasure, at that. And I think there may be more that we haven't seen. These ceremonial rooms were built by the Indians in such a way that they had little cubbyholes in them, something of the size and shape of our telephone booths today. When

they wanted to hide things from their enemies, they'd seal up the cubbyholes with the same kind of plaster that covered the paintings on the wall."

Timmy was listening to the expert with open mouth. Boomer was entranced. Even Lassie looked happy because her young master was pleased.

"I saw the way you opened that passage into the big inner room," Sheriff Casey remarked. "How did you know about that?"

"It was all there in those pictographs on the walls of the main cave," Professor Larkin explained. "They tell a lot about the Indians who used the caves and set up the ceremonial room. I may have to restore some of the details where they've faded out from moisture and the weather. I'd like to keep these caves just the way they are for the time being."

"That's a good idea," agreed Sheriff Casey. "I'll leave a couple of my deputies here now. They'll remain on guard until you have completed your arrangements to preserve this discovery."

"Thank you, Sheriff," Larkin replied.

The party began moving away from the caves, and Lassie barked impatiently. Soon she was leading the way down the trail toward Sentinel Rock, and then to the path that wound down the slope to the wood lot on the Martin farm.

Professor Larkin linked arms with Timmy and Boomer and they strolled along together like the Three Musketeers. Paul and Uncle Petrie smiled as they came along behind.

Tonight would be a big night at the Martin place.

18 PLANS AND PROPHECIES

Ruth Martin was waiting for her family in the yard of the Martin farm. She was ready for them, because the deputies with the prisoners had already come off Kingpin Mountain and had driven away to Capitol City in one of the sheriff's cars.

Lassie was leading the triumphal parade as they came into sight, and Timmy and Boomer were bouncing along the trail behind her as though they had just enjoyed a complete night's rest instead of having endured long, terrifying hours trapped in a cave.

Ruth ran forward and put her arms around the two boys. She smiled as she studied the smudged faces, but like Paul and Uncle Petrie, she wouldn't think of wiping them off. The dirt was a badge of heroism until the boys decided it was time to clean up themselves.

Paul embraced his wife, then introduced her to the real Professor Harry Larkin. Uncle Petrie was talking a mile a minute as he tried to bring Ruth up-to-date on the happenings at the cave.

"They're safe! You're all safe! That's the main thing," Ruth said excitedly.

"We were safe all the time, Mom," Timmy declared.

"I'm sure you were," Ruth said. "But I'll bet there were times when you were scared."

"Some of our biggest heroes have done their best work when they were scared," Professor Larkin pointed out.

Uncle Petrie nodded. "Somewhere I read that these fellows who get the Congressional Medal of Honor usually say something like, 'I was plumb frightened, but I just kept on going.' "

Timmy smiled. Uncle Petrie certainly understood.

"How did you boys find that inner cave?" Paul asked. "I've been wondering about that."

"We followed the bats in there," Boomer explained.

"Bats?" Ruth cried. "You mean there are bats in that cave up there?"

"Thousands of them," Timmy replied promptly. "They go out and feed at night, and they come back just before daylight. You ought to see them, Mom."

Ruth's expression showed clearly that she didn't want to get any closer to those bats than she was right then.

"And you weren't frightened?" she asked unbelievingly.

"We were worried, all right," Boomer admitted. "I was, anyhow. Once when Timmy almost fell into the water—and when we found the bears."

"Bears!" Ruth gave a little scream. "Where are they?"

"Living in the cave," Timmy explained. "Boomer smelled them—said they smelled just like they do in the zoo. So we didn't bother them."

Ruth Martin shook her head. She was sure of one thing. Timmy and Boomer had handled the problems of Kingpin Mountain and the Indian caves much more ably than she would have been able to do.

Lassie was being petted by the sheriff's men before they said good-by and drove off toward Capitol City. Ruth hurried inside to put the finishing touches on dinner for Timmy and Boomer, Paul, Uncle Petrie, and the professor.

They talked about a number of things as they ate. Professor Larkin and the boys had the most to tell. They explained the details of their two imprisonments: one in the farmhouse and the other in the Indian caves.

Lassie was given due credit as the heroine of the whole adventure. She looked up from her feeding bowl alongside the kitchen stove and accepted the praise with calm grace.

"How did the bank bandits make you a prisoner in the first place, Professor?" Timmy asked.

"I guess it was a lot easier than it might have been if I'd been expecting any kind of trouble. They overtook my car on the highway outside of Lewiston while I was on the way to Capitol City, and they ran me off the road. Rowan and Gates held me at gunpoint and took away the car."

"Bill Gates sure acted as though he knew his way around this country," Uncle Petrie broke in. "The sheriff remarked about that on several occasions."

"He did that, all right," Professor Larkin agreed. "I heard him telling Rowan that he used to work on one of the farms at the foot of Kingpin Mountain. That was how he knew about the caves and the trail running from behind the Martin place to the farm on the road to Lewiston."

Paul nodded. "That sounds reasonable, all right. But we owe you an apology for accepting Bill Gates as Professor Larkin without much question."

Professor Larkin shrugged, then smiled as he said, "I guess you had good reasons for doing that too. Gates was a clever fellow—criminals often are. It's too bad they don't use their cleverness in a way that will bring them real success instead of a one-way trip to jail."

"I reckon we were all so anxious to see this Indian expert on the Martin farm that we took him on faith," Uncle Petrie said, putting an arm around Timmy's shoulder. "After all, he did come in an official Government car. It had the insignia on the side and all that. And he knew about the job he was supposed to be doing—that was about all we had a right to expect."

"I'm going to be a lot more careful about things like that in the future," Paul said. "I'll ask for credentials and proper identification. But I guess Bill Gates might have been clever enough to get around that too."

"He would have," the professor agreed. "He took my identification card with my picture on it and substituted one of his own. I don't know what he planned to do about my signature and fingerprint. But if you had been a little more critical with him, it might have speeded things up and saved a lot of trouble for Timmy and Boomer—and for myself."

"Speaking of Boomer . . . ." Paul pointed at Boomer who was slumped far down in his chair. Then he grinned at Timmy, almost asleep in Uncle Petrie's arms.

"I think our boys have had a busy day," Ruth said. "We'd better get them to bed. There'll be plenty of time for new plans and projects in the morning."

Timmy straightened up then, but before he took a step in the direction of his bedroom, he had one last question for Professor Larkin.

"You won't go back up there on Kingpin Mountain again until we can go with you, will you, Professor?"

"Wouldn't think of it," Professor Larkin assured him. "I'm beginning to think that this is going to be the kind of a job where I'll need plenty of help. But I'm going to consider you and Boomer—and Lassie, of course—as my most important helpers."

"Good, good!" Timmy cried happily. "Did you hear that, Lassie?"

Lassie barked briskly. Then she followed Timmy and Boomer into Timmy's bedroom. It looked as if there would be exciting adventures every day from now on and Lassie was ready for them—or she would be after a good night's sleep.

Fiction for Young People

THE RIFLEMAN

THE RESTLESS GUN

WAGON TRAIN

GENE AUTRY
The Ghost Riders

WYATT EARP

GUNSMOKE

ROY ROGERS
The Enchanted Canyon

DALE EVANS
Danger in Crooked Canyon

ROY ROGERS AND DALE EVANS
River of Peril

DRAGNET

BOBBSEY TWINS
Merry Days Indoors and Out
At the Seashore
In the Country

WALTON BOYS
Gold in the Snow
Rapids Ahead

ANNIE OAKLEY
Danger at Diablo
Double Trouble

NOAH CARR, YANKEE FIREBRAND

LEE BAIRD, SON OF DANGER

CIRCUS BOY
Under the Big Top
War on Wheels

HAVE GUN, WILL TRAVEL

MAVERICK

ASSIGNMENT IN SPACE WITH RIP FOSTER

DONNA PARKER
At Cherrydale
Special Agent
On Her Own

TROY NESBIT'S MYSTERY ADVENTURES
The Diamond Cave Mystery
Mystery at Rustlers' Fort

RED RYDER
Adventures at Chimney Rock

RIN TIN TIN
Rinty
Call to Danger
The Ghost Wagon Train

FURY
The Mystery at Trappers' Hole

LASSIE
Mystery at Blackberry Bog
The Secret of the Summer
Forbidden Valley

WALT DISNEY
Spin and Marty
Spin and Marty, Trouble at Triple-R

TRIXIE BELDEN
The Gatehouse Mystery
The Red Trailer Mystery
The Mystery off Glen Road
The Mysterious Visitor
Mystery in Arizona

Adventure! Mystery! Read these exciting stories written especially for young readers